HOPE SPRINGS

HOPE SPRINGS

Jaime Berry

LITTLE, BROWN AND COMPANY

New York   Boston

Copyright © 2021 by Jaime Berry

Cover art copyright © 2021 by Oriol Vidal.
Cover design by Karina Granda.
Cover copyright © 2021 by Hachette Book Group, Inc.

Little, Brown and Company
Hachette Book Group
1290 Avenue of the Americas, New York, NY 10104
Visit us at LBYR.com

First Edition: August 2021

Little, Brown and Company is a division of Hachette Book Group, Inc. The Little, Brown name and logo are trademarks of Hachette Book Group, Inc.

The publisher is not responsible for websites (or their content) that are not owned by the publisher.

Library of Congress Cataloging-in-Publication Data
Names: Berry, Jaime, author.
Title: Hope Springs / Jaime Berry.
Description: First edition. | New York : Little, Brown and Company, 2021. | Audience: Ages 8–12. | Summary: Eleven-year-old crafter Jubilee Johnson's assumptions about her vagabond life, her estranged mother, and her idol, television's perfect crafter Arletta Paisley, start to change after Jubi and her grandmother move to a small Texas town.
Identifiers: LCCN 2020048427 | ISBN 9780316540575 (hardcover) | ISBN 9780316540568 (ebook) | ISBN 9780316540582 (ebook other)
Classification: LCC PZ7.1.B46346 Ho 2021 | DDC [Fic]—dc23
LC record available at https://lccn.loc.gov/2020048427

ISBNs: 978-0-316-54057-5 (hardcover),
978-0-316-54056-8 (ebook)

Printed in the United States of America

LSC-C

Printing 1, 2021

*For my wild,
wonderful boys*

CONTENTS

1. Relocation Rules 1

2. Best Not to Make Best Friends......................... 21

3. Wiggle Room 34

4. Roadblocks 45

5. Faking It 55

6. Blending In... 73

7. Globsnotting Pink Curtains 82

8. Arlene Peavey... 94

9. Good Luck and Wishes Come True............... 108

10. Having It Wrong 119

11. Donut Hole.................................... 135

12. Never to Suffer 151

13. Play It Safe.................................... 169

14. The Rally.................................... 176

15. Top-to-Bottom Right 189

16. Give and Take.. 216

17. Go Fish.. 228

18. Needing to Know 238

19. A Place to Sing.. 252

20. Happily Ever After 259

21. The Hemingway Guy...................................... 267

22. A Perfect Match... 274

23. Hook, Line, and Stinker 282

24. Ready, Set, Rally.. 287

25. The Right Thing 293

26. A Wishing Penny.. 304

27. Staying Put Procedure Number 1.................. 315

Relocation Rules

I knew this day was coming. The final week of sixth grade and the start of summer break creeping up mean prime relocation time. I'd lived with Nan long enough to know the signs.

She'd been in a mood for weeks, and now my new utensil organization system had pushed her grouchiness into a full-out fluster. Every drawer in the kitchen was open and she'd already said three almost-swears: *corn nuts*, *kitty whiskers*, and *bumfuzzle*. I cringed as she tossed a wooden spatula in the Tupperware drawer.

"Nan, if we put things back in the same place we found them, it's easier to find them again," I said.

"Where's the fun in that?" she asked. If Nan was searching for fun in the silverware drawers, we'd be packing up sooner than I thought. Plus, she never put anything in the same place twice, including us.

I'd made sure the maps were out and organized on the table. They sat in my Arletta Paisley® linen expandable snap-top folder next to Nan's kissing squirrels salt and pepper shakers—a gift from our current landlord, Mr. Taft. The shakers sat on opposite ends of the table. I scooted them together for luck.

"Aha! Victory." Nan waved the can opener above her head. Dinner was pretzels and peanut butter with a side of canned peaches. She opened the can and slid the fruit wedges, syrup and all, into two bowls. The foamy soles of her white nurse shoes made a sticky sound on the linoleum as she walked over to the table.

"You read my mind, sugar." She pointed at

the maps with the opener. "This job has fried my nerves. Relocation Rule Number Five-hundred-whatever: Why fight on the battlefield when new fields await?" Some of our rules were tried and true; others, we made up on the spot when the occasion called for it. I wrote them all down in a notebook. We already had nineteen—and counting.

"Let's fold out one of those maps and consider the possibilities," Nan said. "Nothing like a new place to shake things up a little."

According to Nan, she was a born loner but always blessed with a plus-one, first my daddy and now me. Not long after my daddy died, I moved in with Nan, and my momma, well, she just sort of moved on. Nan and I lived in the same apartment in Pleasant View, Tennessee—right outside Nashville—for nearly two whole years. Forever, by Nan's standards. But then Momma started touring so often, there wasn't much point in trying to stay close to her if she was never around. We'd been searching for a place to call home ever since.

"Maybe this time, we'll find the perfect place," I said as I ran my fingers over the folded edges of the maps. "I've got a good feeling."

For years, Nan and I had searched for a place that felt absolutely head-to-toe "just right" perfect. Nan called it a search for substance, but I'd noticed a bit of a pattern. Today, it was a smart-mouthed doctor at the nursing home, last time was my school counselor calling to check on me too often, and the time before that was a traffic cop figuring out Nan's secret to avoiding parking meters. There was always something that led us to getting the maps out.

Shortly after that, we got out too.

Only this time, I had a plan—an Arletta Paisley inspired plan. Even though I was prepared for another move, I felt a little like a squirrel on the inside, all jitters.

Arletta Paisley had her own show on the Hearth & Home Network called *Queen of Neat*. Her sign-off was "Join me next week, because y'all know life can get messy." I liked the idea that I could take my messy life and make something else of it with my own two hands and a little effort. Arletta Paisley was from Hope Springs, Texas, and every word she said came out coated in a thick Texas drawl, sweet but with a little edge, like salted caramel. Maybe Hope Springs would be our perfect place. If it was good enough for Arletta Paisley, then surely it could be good enough for us too.

Nan wouldn't use a computer for our town selections. She said this process required an old-fashioned map and intuition. I'd color-coded our collection of maps with tags made of free paint chips from the hardware store, a practical bit of flair learned from season 4, episode 11: "Neat for Next to Nothing." Next to nothing pretty much summed up our budget.

Since Nan's favorite color was yellow, I'd put a great big honking yellow tag on Texas. Just like magic, she pulled out that map first. She didn't even ask me what the tags meant.

"Texas," Nan said. "Now, a state that big gives us some options." Nan was big on options. For her, choices meant freedom. But for me, I felt most free when I was making something. Arletta's show had turned me into a crafter, someone who could make things by hand. Crafting took skill and creativity, and came with a clear-cut set of directions.

With regular old household items, patience, and imagination, I could create something new. Arletta called it "glamorganizing." But I thought of it as a way to leave a tiny bit of me behind with the people and places we left, and sometimes, a way to take a little something along as a keepsake. All my crafts, from the large-scale collages hanging on the walls to the decorated toilet paper dispenser, were what Nan called "packworthy." The walls and rooms might change, but what was on and in them didn't.

Nan handed me the map, passed a bowl of peaches, and said, "All right, Jubilee, let the search for substance begin."

So, Texas was easy. The tricky part was getting Nan to pick Hope Springs out of all those other towns. I'd dressed for the occasion. Being presentable played a major part in my overall mood. For this very reason, I was not one bit sad to say goodbye to our current apartment with its orangish carpet, watermarked ceiling, and faint smells left by previous owners. I wore a blue gingham skirt I'd sewn myself and an ironed T-shirt, white as a bowl of whole milk.

"Let's see," I said, shaking out the map and spreading it flat on the table. Hope Springs was a little black dot just south of the Arkansas state line, not big enough for the star I was sure it deserved.

Our search officially started when I was seven, about two years after I moved in with Nan. Substance, in her opinion, came with a soulful name and lay south of the Mason-Dixon Line. I'll never forget that first town we decided on together. Calm Waters, Alabama. Back then, I really thought a name mattered. Turned out the only water in Calm Waters was a single muddy pond, and it wasn't so much calm as it was boring. A name like Dull Mud Hole, while a better fit, was probably a bit too honest.

Picking a new place used to feel like an extra exciting game of Go Fish—we were always looking for a match. So, when Nan suggested a move, I'd pack up without a second thought. I knew that, in my "just right" place, I would breathe deep, feeling a loosening of all the things wound up in me, and know I'd found it. The only thing a deep breath did in our current apartment was make me want to pinch my nostrils together. Despite deep cleaning, the shag carpet still smelled like cigar smoke and bacon grease.

"Hmm." I shoved a whole slick slice of peach in my mouth. "This one sounds good," I said, trying to keep the quivery feeling inside out of my voice. "What do you think about Comfort?"

Nan shook her head. "Sounds like an old folks' home."

"Smiley?" I asked.

"Too cutesy." She dipped a pretzel in peanut butter and chomped it. "Something with substance, darlin', not pink ruffles and a tutu." Nan and pink have always had a problematic relationship. She said pink boxed people in, and Nan wasn't one for containment. I personally didn't mind ruffles or pink, or tutus for that matter, but decided now wasn't the time for a disagreement.

"How about Salty, Texas?"

"Maybe if I were in the right mood, but I'm not." She took a drink of her soda, and I took a drink of mine, pretending to study the dickens out of that map.

"Hope Springs?" I asked. I grabbed the edge of my seat, every inch of me pulled up tight as spooled thread. I was ready to come right out and say I wanted to move to Hope Springs, but I knew Nan well enough to know it was better if she thought she had some say in the matter.

Nan closed her eyes, took a slow bite of peach, and got a far-off look. "Hope springs eternal in the human breast," she said, punctuating each word with her forked peach. Nan was an English major before she settled on nursing and hadn't managed to shake it. Our Relocation Rules were mostly a mash-up of lines from her favorite poems, novels, and classic country lyrics. "That's from a poem about how people trust things will work out even when life gets messy." Nan winked at me, clearly wise to my tricks.

I let out a squeal along with all the breaths I'd been holding in. We'd found our new town. "How long have you been on to me?" I asked. Nan was full of quotes but normally steered clear of anything Arletta Paisley.

"As soon as I saw that big yellow tag on the map of Texas, I figured you were up to something. Besides, I've overheard your Arletta Paisley enough to know where she's from." She laughed and, after a bit of quiet, said, "Another letter came for you."

Failing to hide a frown, she laid the envelope down on the map in front of me. Just seeing it turned my mood sour. We only got letters from one person, and the envelopes were always the brightest, deepest, and most entirely pink thing ever created.

Nan rested her hand on mine. Our skin was a little like a paint chip, Nan's fair and mine just a few shades darker. I got most of my looks from Nan and my dad, but my curly hair was all

Momma's doing. Thinking of her letters made me feel like there was something winding up inside me, and that pink envelope wound it one notch tighter. Later, I'd file Momma's letter away with the others I'd never read, slide the lid on the box I kept them in, and then I'd feel better.

Momma wrote the *L* and *K* of her newish name with such long lines and loops, they nearly touched my name down in the center of the envelope. She changed names almost as often as we changed addresses. Before she became a touring country singer, her real name was Alexandra Kirkson, and then it was Alexandra Johnson when she married my dad. Now, she went by Lexie Kirk. After she visited for Christmas, Mr. Taft admitted he'd never heard of her. He wasn't the only one.

Momma only had two songs that ever got any airtime: "Wait Just a Little Bit Longer" and "Even Donuts Have Holes." Her donut song was picked up by a national donut chain and was her "big money hit." I don't know about big, but that money was sure gone fast. Currently, she tours as a backup singer for country music star Brent Chisholm. Even Mr. Taft had heard of Brent Chisholm.

Every month, two envelopes arrived: one for Nan and one for me. I knew Nan opened hers because I'd seen the check on the kitchen counter. Mine always stayed sealed.

The checks were written in the squat, neat print of Momma's manager, Wynn. Wynn, my dad, and my mom were all friends in high school, and he'd been her manager since they were both teenagers. He came with Momma at Christmas, dressed in embroidered Western shirts and pointy-toed leather boots. After my dad died and before I moved in with Nan, he'd tried to step in. Maybe he thought love worked like a Ping-Pong ball and would bounce around between the three of us. In particular, I'm pretty sure he hoped some of Momma's love would bounce around to him.

"I'll call her later. We'll get her our new address as soon as we have it," Nan said and gave my hand a squeeze.

"That's okay. I'll do it." Nan raised an eyebrow. I didn't often offer to call Momma. "What? I haven't talked to her in months," I said. She nodded and slid her cell phone across the table. I knew exactly the last time I'd talked to Momma. It was five months ago on my eleventh birthday, and I knew from the screen on Nan's phone that the call lasted only six minutes and thirteen seconds. She lived in Dallas, and though she was rarely there, it was only a day's drive. A drive she hardly ever made.

I scrolled through Nan's contacts while she cleaned up. Momma didn't have any room to criticize a person moving too often, but it hadn't kept her quiet the last time we packed up. This time, it was completely my idea, and I planned on telling her so.

"Hey, Jubi! Saw Nan's number, figured it was you, so I picked up." It was Wynn. "Everything okay?"

"Everything's fine." It was just like him to dive right in with questions even though I'd called to talk to Momma. Nan banged some dishes around. I got up and walked down our short hallway toward my room. "Is Momma there?"

"She's currently in the recording booth!" Wynn said it all excited, like she was walking on the moon or something. "So, what's up?" he asked after my unimpressed silence.

"Just checking in. Could you have her call me back?" I asked.

"Sure. Probably be at least half an hour before she wraps this up."

"Great. Thanks." I hung up before he could press for more information.

That thirty minutes turned into an hour, and that hour then dragged into two. By the time I got ready for bed, Momma still hadn't called back. My brain knew better than to think she would change more than her name, but my stupid heart kept hoping. That's the thing about a second chance—it doesn't mean much when the person wasted the first one. Plus, I'd learned from Nan that even one shot was sometimes one too many.

Nan knocked and entered my room. She glanced down at the unopened letter and sat on the edge of my bed.

"What'd your momma have to say?" she asked. "We'll be in the same state, even closer than we are now. She'll like that."

"Nothing," I said. "She had nothing to say." Nan waited for me to say more, but I didn't.

"You know, Van Gogh said something like, 'The more you love, the more you suffer.'" Recently, Nan had worked some famous artists' quotes into her rotation for my benefit.

"Didn't he also cut his ear off and mail it to a lady?" I asked.

"So, maybe not the best person to get advice from, huh?" she agreed, and we both laughed. Then she looked up at the old watermark left from a long-ago leak above my bed. "You sure you're ready to say goodbye to this palace?"

I nodded. "I'm sure."

She patted my leg before rising to leave. I knew she thought I'd talked to Momma, but

Momma could hardly be mad about our moving if she couldn't be bothered to return a phone call.

"We'll start packing first thing," Nan said, blew a kiss, and shut my door.

I snatched Momma's letter off my bed and thought about tearing it in half. Instead, I slid the box out, shoved the crumpled envelope inside with the others, and with a kick, sent the box sliding back under my bed. Whatever Momma had to tell me that she couldn't come out and say in person could go on and wait just a little bit longer, like her song suggested.

Hope Springs was going to be my perfect place; I just knew it. I wasn't about to let Momma ruin my good mood. Packing always took my mind off things. So, I hopped up and got to work.

I didn't have much to take. Relocation Rule Number 4: It's easier to say goodbye if there's not much to say goodbye to. We didn't need extra things. But each month, that stupid box of pink letters from Momma got fuller, and each time we moved, I thought about leaving it behind. Maybe leaving things behind ran in my family.

When I'd wait for the school bus in the mornings, Mr. Taft and I fed the squirrels together. Starting next week, Mr. Taft would be feeding the squirrels on his own. Another person we'd leave behind, and I knew he'd miss us. He seemed even more alone than Nan and me.

I grabbed two thick sheets of card stock. My Caring Critter Card would do the trick. It was my staple thank-you, get well soon, any holiday, and most often goodbye card and could be modified to almost any animal. I made an owl for Ms. Landry, my fourth-grade teacher. After I told her I only had two more days before we moved, she cried a flood. The owl held a heart, and on it I wrote, "You're a hoot" in my neatest cursive, but really, she wasn't all that funny. In fact, she cried a lot.

As I took out the other crafting supplies I'd need, I could hear Arletta's voice in my head. "Nothing says you care like a handmade gift." I set everything out, nice and neat and ready for a close-up, just like Arletta always did. After going over the supplies, she'd say, "Now, let me talk you through it." I started on the card and let Arletta's voice and the act of making something soothe my feelings.

I made Mr. Taft's card into a squirrel, and when I finished, I wrote "I'm nuts about you" on the heart, though that wasn't all that true either.

MR. TAFT'S CARING CRITTER CARD

Level: Beginner

Supplies:

- ❋ 2 5-inch by 7-inch pieces of card stock or construction paper cut to the right size would also do in a pinch

- ❋ 2 googly eyes (though I think handmade eyes from nice paper look a bit more mature)

- ❋ Red construction paper

Tools:

- ❋ Scissors

- ❋ Glue stick

- ❋ Black marker

Directions:

1. Cut the corners off one of the 5-inch sides of the card and fold that end a quarter of the way down, making the face of the squirrel.

2. Stick on googly or handmade eyes. Draw a mouth and nose using the marker.

3. Use the other card to cut out a tail, ears, and two paws (or any other features the critter of your choosing might have).

4. Glue the tail on the back so it sticks out to the side or up behind the head.

5. Using the red paper, cut out a small heart about three inches across. Glue the heart on the squirrel's stomach and then glue the two paws on the sides.

6. Be sure to write a critter-themed message on the heart (sincerity isn't necessary, but a hint of the truth sure can go a long way).

2

Best Not to Make Best Friends

School ended on a Wednesday. We packed all our worldly belongings into Nan's old hatchback on Thursday and were on the road first thing Friday morning. After four hours of driving, sandwiched by yellowed cow pastures on each side, we were almost there.

"In six miles, exit left," Nan's GPS interrupted during her rotation of Willie Nelson and Dolly Parton songs. She may not rely on modern technology to find our new towns, but she sure did to drive there.

The little dot labeled Hope Springs crept closer and closer. I smoothed my twice-ironed skirt. Try as I might, I wasn't able to smooth out my nerves or squish down my high expectations.

As we drove past an acre of flattened land and the makings of a huge building, my breath caught. It was all I could do to gasp and point. A billboard plastered with Arletta Paisley's face smiled down like a Texan angel sent from above just for me. Under her face were the words SMARTMART SUPERSTORE OPENING SOON. Already, I had a good feeling about Hope Springs, and that billboard was like Arletta Paisley herself saying, "Jubilee, darlin', I'm so glad you came."

Nan laughed. "Looks like you've got your own personal meet-and-greet committee."

Arletta Paisley had recently become the national spokesperson for SmartMart, and with both of them greeting me at the city limits, I felt double welcomed. SmartMart was the same in every town. I always knew where to find exactly what I wanted, and what I wanted was normally in the back of the store, where Arletta Paisley's housewares lined the shelves. Overstuffed pillows, fluffy bath mats, floral-print shower curtains, pastel comforter sets, four-hundred-thread-count cotton sheets, and dishes, all in the calm shades of baby nurseries. Walking the aisles, I almost felt embraced.

Nan and I always did a drive-through in a new town, but our Hope Springs exploration didn't last long because there wasn't much to drive through. There was only one middle school, one high school, one biggish grocery store, and one run-down city pool, but about one million beauty parlors and churches. The library was the smallest one I'd ever seen, and the community center wasn't much bigger. Another surprise was that Hope Springs, on first inspection, didn't have any sign, statue, or other significant marker dedicated to Arletta Paisley. I didn't even see anyone carrying one of her signature handbags or wearing a *Queen of Neat* T-shirt like the one I had folded up tight and tidy in my suitcase.

"Well, let's see what we've got," Nan said as we parked in front of City Hall. Our first day of a new move always started at City Hall. Nan said it was the fastest way to get settled into a new town. She never worried about getting a job. As a certified nursing assistant, or a CNA for short, she figured there'd never be a shortage of sick folks needing assistance.

Downtown consisted of two intersecting streets, Main Street and High Street, separated by a single flashing stoplight and no traffic. Not a single moving car.

Hope Springs's City Hall was a two-story brick building with tall white columns and pairs of paint-peeled shutters on every window. In front, there was a stone well with a commemorative plaque. *Finally*, I thought and walked up to it, wondering what the heck a well had to do with Arletta Paisley.

The plaque read:

THIS WELL IS DEDICATED TO THE COURAGEOUS PIONEERS WHO SETTLED THIS TOWN IN THE YEAR 1836. DESPITE SEEMINGLY INSURMOUNTABLE HARDSHIP, INCLUDING THE DEVASTATING DROUGHT OF 1840, THESE BRAVE INDIVIDUALS RISKED THEIR LIVES TO LAY THE FOUNDATION FOR THE COMMUNITY THAT EXISTS TODAY. THEIR TIRELESS EFFORTS IN THE FACE OF ADVERSITY HAVE GIVEN US ALL A TREASURE WORTH MORE THAN GOLD—A HOME. WHILE THE SPRING IS NO MORE, LET THIS WELL BE A REMINDER THAT HOPE SPRINGS ETERNAL.

Nan came and stood behind me, reading over my shoulder. "I'll be," she mumbled. "Guess that means there's no spring in Hope Springs." She chuckled all the way to the foot of the steps. "You coming?"

I didn't think too much of fate or fortunes, but a dried-up spring sure didn't seem like a great start. I closed my eyes and took deep gulps of air, trying to breathe in the place. No tingling, no goose bumps, not even a hint of perfection whatsoever. The only thing I felt was a strong urge to sweep the steps.

With my eyes still closed, I tried to picture

that billboard again. I tried to reclaim that hopeful feeling I'd had just minutes before. I tried to ignore the fact that so far Hope Springs was falling a little short of what I'd hoped for.

"Nan, you mind if I wait here?" I sighed and plopped down on the first step, worried we'd made our way into another dead-end, boring, waste of time, dusty mudhole of a town, with another move not too far off.

"Sure, hon. But don't wander." She took the steps two at a time, her wooden wedges making a dull clomp to match my mood.

Nan turned and gave me a silly two-thumbs-up before going in. I prayed she found somewhere decent for us to live. She tended to trust her gut when it came to our rentals, and history had proven her gut wasn't to be trusted.

As I sat staring down the empty Main Street, the heat pressed on me until sweat trickled down my back. The stoplight creaked and swung in the slight breeze. I stood, stomped back over to the well, and dug around in my bag for a penny. Surely, that billboard meant something. I held my coin out, ready to wish that this place would be it, would be the perfect place we'd been searching for. With that penny balanced on my nail, waiting for a flip, I thought too long on all the things I might wish for and froze.

Nan was my father's mother. He'd died in a motorcycle accident when I was four. I only had two clear memories of him. One was of a Big Bird birthday cake and my dad singing loud, Nan and Momma laughing and covering their ears. The other was of his short black hair and how it felt rough and soft at the same time, like crushed velvet. All I knew of him was from Nan's stories. Sometimes, I thought losing him was harder for her because she remembered so much more, and because the motorcycle had been a hand-me-down present from her.

Nan hadn't been on a motorcycle since Daddy died, but she sure hadn't settled down any either. Other grandmothers with their sensible shoes, poufs of white hair, and flowery smells were nothing like Nan. She kept her hair cropped short and dyed jet black and smelled sharp and clean like cut grass. Though Nan's biker days were behind her, the look stuck. She had a flair for fashion and makeup that was best left untapped.

I looked up to see a boy in a Texas Rangers hat watching me from across the street. He gave me a little wave, turned, and took off down Main Street before I had a chance to wave back. With the coin still waiting on my finger, I looked down into that empty well and thought about that kid I'd just seen, and how many new kids I'd met and then left behind. I wanted Nan and me to find a home, but really, the one thing I truly wanted was to wish that motorcycle out of existence. But the idea of my wish getting mixed up with hundreds and hundreds of strangers' hopes made me drop the penny back into my purse.

"Hey, don't fall in. There's no water down there." A girl my age came bouncing down the steps. Her knees were speckled with scabs, and her hair was a jumble of short dark curls thick enough to hide Easter eggs. "I'm Abby," she said. "Abby Standridge. My mom's the mayor. I'm not bragging. Just telling you before you hear it from someone else. Small town—everybody talks."

Abby's shorts were spattered with paint stains, and the pocket of her T-shirt was half torn off. She didn't look a bit like the perfectly pressed, ready-for-Sunday-school politicians' kids I'd seen on TV.

"I'm Jubilee. Nan and I just moved here." I flicked a tattered leaf off my skirt.

"I know. I met your grandma inside at Housing and Development. Which is what my mom calls Mrs. Fisher, the receptionist. They were talking about Mrs. Burgess's old house. It's nice. There's a pond nearby that's full of catfish." She looked at me like she expected an invitation. Fishing was not my idea of a good time, or even a halfway decent time. Besides that, it sounded like a best friends' activity.

All last year, I'd held strongly to Relocation Rule Number 6: It's best not to make best friends.

I'd made that mistake once before, and I wasn't about to do it again.

"I don't think we brought my fishing pole." I'd never in my life laid eyes on a real fishing pole, but I'd learned from Nan that, when it came to strangers, less truth meant less trouble.

"I live right down the road from the old Burgess place. You can't miss my house; it's big, old, and bright yellow. If you want, you could ride your bike over. Maybe I can even find an extra rod," she offered. Before I could answer, she waved and ran back up the steps.

"I don't think we brought my bike either!" I yelled after her.

While Abby seemed nice enough, it turned out we had different taste in extracurricular activities, and houses too. The Burgess place was anything but nice. The building sat at the end of a dirt driveway that erupted in plumes of dust at the sight of a car tire. One set of shutters was missing and the other hung lopsided, like the whole house had been smacked catawampus.

Out in a field, I could see the glassy top of a large pond of murky green water. The banks rose up thick with weeds, and the water seemed to suck in the sun rather than reflect it. If it was full of anything, it'd be snakes and maybe a swamp monster or two.

Nan killed the engine. We sat while the dust settled and stared for a minute.

"Well, it's a step up from the apartment complex," she said. "I thought a house would be nice for a change. It's furnished too. Had to give a deposit, plus first and last months' rent for the year. But we'll make do." That was code for she'd spent all or most of our money. "Why not start off with the best?"

I studied the house. If this was the best, I needed to adjust my expectations. The perfect place didn't *necessarily* mean the place we lived in. So, I opened my car door and tried to be open-minded.

Nan must have sensed my skepticism. "We'll make it work. 'Creativity takes courage.' Henri

Matisse." She walked over to my side of the car, grabbed my hand, and pulled me forward.

The walk to the porch coated my new white canvas slip-ons in a thin layer of orange dirt. While Nan fiddled with the keys, the wind kicked up and, just as she unlocked the door, a sand-filled gust blew right in our faces. We stepped inside. Nan gasped and dropped the bags in the middle of the living room.

"Holy horseradish," she whispered. She turned in a slow circle, her mouth hanging open as she took it all in. Every single piece of furniture was covered in pink fabric—the kitchen cabinets were painted pink, the wood floors were covered in pink patterned rugs, and the couch was worn pink velvet. "Jubilee, am I dreaming?" It took every inch of my self-control to keep from laughing, but then Nan looked at me all wide-eyed, and we busted into a fit of giggles.

I grabbed her hand. One thing I'd learned from Arletta was that a true crafter didn't just see what was in front of them; they saw possibilities. I wasn't ready to give up on Hope Springs, and I wouldn't let Nan do it either. "Don't worry. Like you said, with a bit of courage, creativity and fifteen"—I eyed the pink and mauve striped drapes in the living room—"thirty-five yards of upholstery fabric, anything is possible." A couch cover wasn't an easy thing to whip up, but sometimes the glamorganizing way of life wasn't for the faint of heart.

3

Wiggle Room

Nan and I left our bags where they landed and headed back to town. We stopped at the lonesome traffic light and scanned Main Street. Next to the post office stood a store called the Fabric Barn.

We parked and I peered through the dusty store window. "Well, it looks like this is it. We might as well go in," I said.

Inside, the store was about as tidy as an actual barn and didn't smell much better. Bolts of fabric lined aisles in no apparent order, and some weren't even on a rack but propped up against the wall. Knitting supplies were mixed with quilting supplies, a scissors display was smack in the middle of a rack of corduroy, and the aisles turned and twisted rather than running in straight lines.

There was a cutting table marked up with scratches and gouges next to a register, though getting there was like navigating a Halloween corn maze. Behind the counter sat a lady with a long braid of white hair trailing over one shoulder. Her face was buried in a romance novel titled *My General Forever*, and a large snoring bulldog lay curled in a pile of wrinkled skin at her feet.

Nan cleared her throat, and instead of looking up, the woman raised her index finger and turned the page. When she finished, she clutched the book to her chest and said, "That General Maldonado is a real scoundrel. I personally can't get enough of him." She held out her hand to Nan. "Holly Paine. Nice to meet you both."

Nan shook her hand and said, "I'm Nannette Johnson and this is my granddaughter, Jubilee."

Holly nodded and removed her reading glasses. "Old Mrs. Burgess was a real fan of pink. She singlehandedly kept me in business my first year." She laughed at our dumbfounded expressions. "Don't look so shocked. News travels fast in Hope Springs." The bulldog shook his face, curled up again with his back facing us, and then a horrible smell wafted up.

"Oh my," Nan said and fanned the air. I fought the urge to hold my nose.

"Sorry about that. It's Rayburn. He's got a touch of gas," Holly whispered and pointed to the bulldog as though he might be offended if he overheard. She looked me up and down. "Well, aren't you neat as a box pleat. Got any fabrics in mind today?" she asked.

I felt myself blush at the compliment and asked, "Where's your cotton canvas?"

"Some along the back wall and scattered in aisles three, four, and six," Holly answered with a wave of her hand. "In other words, all over. Might be easier if I just showed you." She came out from behind the register and led me to the fabric bolts, stacks of solids mixed with prints, cottons with satins, and linen with corduroys. I couldn't figure how she found anything but the bulldog. Finding him only required a sense of smell.

"What about this gray for the sofa cover and some prints in yellow for the curtains and the pillows?" I asked Nan.

But it was Holly who nodded and said, "That'd look real nice."

"Maybe something in a vintage-looking print for the kitchen chairs and the window over the sink?" I added.

Again, Holly Paine was right beside me, nodding like a bobblehead. "I know just the one," she said, and next thing I knew, she had me by the hand, dragging me up one aisle and down the other. She yelled over her shoulder to Nan, "This girl knows fabric!"

"She knows more than fabric. She's the most creative person I've ever met. Jubilee can make something beautiful out of an empty bottle and an old toothbrush," Nan said.

Holly chuckled and pulled out a dusty bolt of fabric printed with bright yellow chrysanthemums. "What about this? It isn't a reproduction. This is the real deal, circa 1975. Still here after all these years and not faded a bit." She wiggled her eyebrows. "Kind of like me."

Nan looked at her and said, "'Youth has no age.' Pablo Picasso."

"Oh, I like that," Holly said.

"And I love that fabric," Nan said.

"Me too," I agreed. "Vintage fabrics are my favorite."

"Well, you'll find plenty of vintage in here." Holly laughed. "I think some of these patterns are as old as I am."

She motioned to a large shelf in the middle of the store. It was more like a stack of shelves stuffed full of pattern envelopes, some so old they'd yellowed along the edges. I walked over and pulled one out. I loved looking at patterns; each one with alteration ideas was a solid set of instructions packed with possibilities.

Nan picked up one advertising "10 great

looks with one easy pattern!" and said, "It's like an envelope full of options. You want it?"

Almost more than anything else, Nan liked to have options.

I nodded, and while Nan went up to the register, I went back to perusing. One pattern had a little girl younger than me sitting in the lap of an older girl, probably meant to be her sister. A whole section was stuffed with matching outfits—mother-daughter, sisters, maybe even cousins. The patterns for kids all seemed to hint at family, and not a single one looked like me and Nan.

We ended up with more fabric than we could carry out ourselves, and Holly gave us two yards of the mum fabric for free. After helping us load the car, she leaned her head in the window and said, "You know, Jubilee, I have a few jobs I could use some help with. You ever have any free time, and if it's all right with you, Nan, I'd love the company and the extra pair of hands. I'll pay you, of course, as long as I've got consent from your guardian."

Nan nodded and I said, "Sure, I'll think about it." Nan had taught me to be cautious when it came to commitments. Together, we'd come up with Relocation Rule Number 11: Always leave yourself some wiggle room. If I didn't make any promises, then I wouldn't have to break them later.

Once the windows were up and we were back on the road, Nan hummed along to Patsy Cline. "Holly seems nice," I said.

"Mmm-huh," Nan mumbled. She looked at me. "I guess she was, but I've got the only friend I need right here. Relocation Rule Number One: When it comes down to it, it's just the two of us. Me and my Jubilee." Nan sang that last bit every time.

I smiled like always, but something about it bothered me. I'd never really questioned Nan much about our moving. But I was beginning to wonder if she was really searching for the perfect place... or just searching? Did she ever truly think we'd settle down somewhere? And how were we ever going to find a perfect place if she never gave anywhere or anyone a chance?

The more I thought about our first Relocation Rule, the more it rubbed me wrong, and the more "just the two of us" felt like one away from alone.

There was something about Holly Paine and the Fabric Barn. The mess there felt disordered, for sure, but it also felt different—comfortable almost. When Holly walked down the aisles, I'd noticed she ran her fingertips lightly across the bolts of fabric. I wanted to do the same thing, reach out and touch all that possibility waiting to be unrolled and made into something.

By the time we pulled into our new driveway, I'd decided to make Holly Paine some lemon-scented room deodorizer in a mason jar from Arletta Paisley's Homemade Home Scents week. I'd never made anyone something after only just meeting them, but Holly and Rayburn seemed in desperate and immediate need of some subtle glamorganizing.

HOLLY PAINE'S LEMON-SCENTED JELLY JAR ROOM DEODORIZER

Level: Advanced

Supplies*:

* 2 lemons

* 1-pint glass mason jar (really any glass jar will do) with lid

* 3 sprigs fresh rosemary

* 1 teaspoon vanilla extract

* 1 square fabric swatch, large enough to cover the lid

* Small card

* ½ yard grosgrain ribbon, plus more if decorating the lid

* For a stronger scent, double the amount of lemon, rosemary, and vanilla. Recommended for Rayburn or other gassy companions, animal or otherwise.

Tools:

* Kitchen knife (have a parent or guardian around for this)

* Glue stick

* Scissors

* Hole punch

Directions:

1. Slice lemons ½-inch thick and arrange in the jar with sprigs of rosemary (equally spacing the rosemary against the jar and pushing the lemons onto them makes a nice pattern).

2. Pour in the vanilla extract and add water and fill to the top.

3. Center and glue the fabric swatch onto the lid; for extra glamour, wrap a ribbon around the edge.

4. Use a pen to write the instructions on the card.**

5. Punch a hole in the corner of the card, run the ribbon through, and tie it onto the jar in a bow.

** Instructions to be written on the card: Pour the contents into an appropriate container and put it on the stovetop, on a hot plate, in a Crock-pot, or in a potpourri cooker over low heat. As the water evaporates, add more.

4

Roadblocks

All Friday afternoon, Nan and I sewed, rolled up rugs, and packed as much pink as we could into the old shed in the backyard. The kitchen cabinets, slathered in a bold coat of Pepto-Bismol pink, were a real problem. Hard to change and even harder to leave alone.

"Maybe we could cover the cabinet fronts with contact paper or fabric. Or I could stencil another color over the front. I don't think I can repaint a whole kitchen. Can we even change the cabinets?" I opened a drawer full of rubber bands, old batteries, rusted spoons, and what I hoped was a dried-up raisin. I slammed the drawer shut. "I'm going to have bad dreams about that drawer."

"Oh now, don't overreact. You'll think of something. You always come up with a project that makes our place better. And I can help. But until then, I vote we eat on the couch and cook wearing a blindfold," Nan said.

Her cooking started with a can opener and ended with a microwave—blindfolded or not, it couldn't get much worse. Nan wasn't always the best problem solver. She relied heavily on Relocation Rule Number 13: When faced with a roadblock, get off the road. Some of the rules had a double dose of Nan and only a sprinkle of me. Matter of fact, I liked a challenge—liked to take something and fix it up. But I did need a break from that kitchen. It was hard to see many opportunities when faced with floor-to-ceiling pink cabinets and drawers teeming with the stuff of nightmares.

"I think I might work in my room for a while," I said.

My bedroom had plenty of pink, but I didn't mind, because next to it was old Mrs. Burgess's quilting room (also pink). It was empty except for built-ins all along one wall and a long table perfect for working on projects. I never in a million years thought I'd have my very own crafting room. All thoughts of the kitchen swept clean out of my brain as soon as I walked down the hall.

For the rest of the evening, I unpacked and arranged my supplies. There was a whole box of dusty mason jars in the shed. After some cleaning, they sparkled and held small knickknacks labeled with card stock tags. I'd seen the exact same thing in Arletta Paisley's slightly blurry background. When Nan knocked on the door and asked if I wanted frozen pizza or a can of soup for dinner, I went with the soup just so I could drink it down and get back to work.

Arletta Paisley's show was filmed in her house, mostly in the kitchen or her craft room.

Both were bright white with touches of aqua and pale lemon yellow. Those rooms stayed the same from month to month and felt more like home to me than any of the places Nan and I'd actually lived. As I worked, the shelves slowly filled, and by the time night rolled around, I had a feeling that maybe this truly was it; maybe this place could be different than all the others. That feeling seemed to expand, spreading over me every time I stepped back to look over my work.

The next morning, all I wanted to do was stretch out flat on the couch, watch a few hours of the Hearth & Home Network, and then get back to my craft room. Arletta Paisley's summer season premiere was only a few days away, and H & H was showing a heavy rotation of reruns to build excitement about the new show.

I hopped out of bed, skipped to the living room, and set up my notebook, my sharpened Ticonderogas (three: one to use, one if the other broke, and one just in case), and my two ink pens—a special one for jotting quotes from Arletta and one for calligraphy—and a highlighter, for extra emphasis. Even though I'd seen the episodes before, I knew they were full of hidden gems. Besides, a good idea sometimes deserved to be written down twice.

During a commercial break, I hustled to the hall bathroom to wet and comb antifrizz foam through my hair. My hair resisted my organization efforts almost as much as Nan. While I tried to smooth some final flyaways, Arletta Paisley's commercial echoed down the hall. I didn't have to be there to picture it; I had the whole thing memorized. She smiled, nodded her big blonde hair, and said, "Join me for a whole new season of *Queen of Neat*, because y'all know life can get messy." Then she winked one of her deep lake-blue eyes. Everything about her seemed tranquil and soothing, pillowy almost, and gave me a feeling I could sink into.

Nan once joked and called Arletta Paisley my "TV momma." A joke I did not find all that funny, maybe because there was too much truth in it. My real mom was Arletta Paisley's opposite. Momma, with her long dark curls and sharp angles. She was always thin, always beautiful, and always gone. It'd been days since I'd called her but still no call back, no text, no nothing.

On my tenth birthday, Momma promised to drive down and take me out to dinner, just the two of us. But then a spot for a singer opened up at a club in Austin, Texas. So she drove there instead. I knew better than to count on her for anything other than a disappointment. But knowing better didn't keep my heart from hoping things might change.

I ran my palm coated with cream over my hair and hoped it might get rid of frizz along with all mom-related thoughts.

We hadn't yet started sewing the couch cover, but I'd cut out the pieces, some still fastened to the cushions. I straightened my supplies on the coffee table and sat, careful to avoid the pins, and smiled at the idea that Arletta would be the first friend I welcomed into my new place. As I settled in, a knock sounded at the door.

On our small slab porch stood Abby Standridge, dressed like a carpenter, hair as big as an azalea bush, and holding two fishing poles. "Hi. Brought an extra. The pond's not too far a walk from here."

"I-I'm not really dressed for fishing," I stammered. I wore a floral summer dress Nan had helped me sew from a pattern last year. Nan's help was mostly supervisory in nature. The dress was a little small and fish slime wouldn't be an improvement. Arletta's intro music played in the background.

"Well, just throw on some shorts. Normally, I ask my friend Colton, but he can't today," Abby said.

To me, a day was mapped out and dressed for; I called it my POD—plan of the day. Fishing wasn't part of that itinerary. I had to tackle a whole couch cover and still wanted to work on my craft room.

Plus, I did not "throw" on anything.

A long "ummm" was all I could manage before Nan hollered from the kitchen, "Jubilee, who's there?"

Nan walked behind me mumbling something

about neighbors as the camera zoomed in on Arletta wearing a chambray denim shirtdress and sitting at a worn oak table. Season 1, episode 8: "Hand-Lettering from the Heart."

"Nice to see you again, Ms. Johnson," Abby said.

Nan and I stared at Abby.

"Well." Nan looked at me. "Guess we better invite your new friend in."

My mind was hand-lettering a variety of *get lost* messages, but my mouth said, "Come on in."

Breakfast was instant oatmeal and yogurt spooned from individual containers into a large lumpy bowl Nan and I had made in a "Mom and Me" pottery class. Nan occasionally joined in on my crafting. But solo crafting was more my thing. I took do-it-yourself more literally than most.

Abby came right in and sat down at the table. "Y'all made some changes. Old Mrs. Burgess sure had a thing for pink. She wore it head to toe. Even her hair was a touch pink. But you gotta respect a person who has a passion."

Nan and I stared at Abby again. Nan cleared her throat. "I guess that's true. I always like a person who isn't afraid to be themselves."

Abby nodded. "Me too." She looked over at me and flashed a big smile. There was no easy way to get out of this. Nan answered my pleading look with a discreet shrug. Sometimes she wasn't any help at all. Seemed like I was about to experience the joys of fishing, whether I really wanted to or not.

"Guess I'll go change." I left the kitchen, turning off the TV with a stifled sigh. By the time I returned from my room, wearing my oldest T-shirt and cutoffs, Abby had a bowl in front of her and a napkin on her lap, and she and Nan were visiting like old friends.

"Can I interest you in some miniature marshmallows for your oatmeal?" Nan asked.

"Absolutely," Abby said.

"I personally think no meal's complete without them," Nan said.

"I can get behind that idea," Abby agreed.

"What do you two have planned?" Nan asked.

"I was going to take Jubilee fishing over at Miss Esther's pond. She's down the road and doesn't mind, long as I call her first." Abby blew on a lumpy spoonful of oatmeal.

Nan almost spit out her coffee. "My Jubilee? Going fishing? Well, that's a new one." She gave me a peck on the head and said, "Fish, I love you and respect you very much. But I will kill you dead before this day ends."

Abby and I both stared at her, swinging a spoon like it was a sword and staring out the kitchen window. "Hemingway? *The Old Man and the Sea*? Good grease-gravy, what do they teach you kids at school?" That Hemingway guy was one of Nan's favorites and inspired a few of our best Relocation Rules. He must have been quick to pack up and move along too.

Abby smiled and raised an eyebrow at me. I shrugged, trying not to blush.

New Private Relocation Rule: Keep all potential friends away from Nan.

5

Faking It

The grass in our new yard was as brown and crunchy as peanut brittle. Abby practically skipped toward that sickly looking pond. I stumbled along behind her, careful to avoid the dust she kicked up, and struggling to steady a flutter of growing nerves. I didn't know a thing about fishing, and I hadn't been on a one-on-one outing with a friend in over a year.

"Nan's your grandma, right?" Abby asked when we reached the end of the driveway.

I nodded. My stomach seemed to be tying

itself in knots. Maybe that was it—I could fake a stomachache and be back on the couch in no time.

"She sure isn't like my gram," Abby said. "Gram kind of smells like lemon-scented mothballs and licks napkins to wipe off my face. It's disgusting."

If Nan ever tried to lick me, I'd think her mind had turned to marshmallow fluff.

"Her main interests are baking and church. She thinks her piecrust recipe is a personal gift from Jesus himself. If you ask me, the crust is the worst part of a pie. Nan cook much?"

I gave her a look. After all, she'd just eaten one of Nan's best breakfasts, and we both laughed. I'd hold on to my stomachache excuse for now, see how things went, and if I wasn't having fun in ten minutes, then I'd use it. Abby turned at the end of our drive and jumped over the ditch that ran by the side of the road. She walked up to a barbed-wire fence. Then she stuck her foot on the bottom row of wire and pulled up the top row, making a wide space.

"Well, go on through," she said.

"You want me to go through there?" I asked. "Isn't there a gate somewhere?"

"Come on. You can do it," she said. She pulled the wires wider and motioned with her head.

Nan and I had a Relocation Rule for this kind of predicament: When something is totally new, pretend it isn't. I always had to fake it a little bit, and then when we moved, I had to fake it all over again with a whole new set of people. But things didn't have to be new all the time if we'd stick around long enough for something to happen more than once. For Nan, uncertainty meant adventure and opportunity. But for me, uncertainty was starting to feel like I could never count on anything to stay the same.

I looked at Abby, and she gave me a big smile and encouraging nod. I leaned down and squeezed through, careful to avoid the barbs. When I straightened on the other side, a breeze whipped my hair and I felt a touch braver than I had just seconds before.

Once, on a winter field trip to the Oklahoma

state capital, I stepped in an icy puddle. My teacher, Mrs. Lester, had a garbage bag full of extra clothes she took on bus trips. She gave me a pair of gym socks to wear. They were clean but worn and pilled at the heel. It was too cold to say no, but putting them on almost made me gag. Lately, that's what a new town felt like—sliding my foot into somebody else's old gym sock.

I held the fence open for Abby like she'd done for me. She smiled again, stepped through in one quick motion, stood, and took off toward a beaten trail.

"Last year, I caught a six-and-a-half-pound bass at the Family Pairs Bass Tournament. Used to be called the Father-Son Bass Roundup, but Mom caused a fuss until they changed it. I came in second place to Mr. Meacham. He beat me by two-tenths of a pound. Mr. Meacham owns Meacham Auto Repair and wears overalls every day. Rumor is, that's all he wears. Built-in air-conditioning."

I laughed and said, "Gross."

"Even grosser if you know Mr. Meacham."

Abby shuddered, then pointed to an outcrop of rocks. "Steer clear. Saw a rattlesnake there last week."

I choked on another laugh about Mr. Meacham and walked closer to Abby.

"I'm a member of the Junior Bassmasters Club. You could join too, if you want." She skipped forward like rattlesnakes were as harmless as dandelions.

"There's a club for fishing?" I asked. She gave me a look like I'd asked if the sun was made of yellow chiffon.

"Course there is. There're clubs for about anything. Fishing can be simple, but being really good is complicated," she said. "But you don't have to be really good to join Bassmasters. You just have to love to fish."

Well, that disqualified me on both counts. Though, I'd seen enough paper-plate crafts and lumpy decoupage to know exactly what she meant about the difference between a hobby and a skill.

The pond looked even worse up close. The

bank was a muddy slope covered in ragged weeds. Bugs as big as hummingbirds zipped on and off the water while little ones swarmed in small dark clouds. And the smell of mud, mold, and wet rot was thick enough to stick.

I stopped short of an old dock, while Abby hopped over missing planks, walked to the end of it, took off her backpack, and settled down on one of the potentially rotted boards.

"You coming?" she asked

I stepped on a plank that creaked with my weight and hesitated. "Will it hold both of us?"

"Sure it will. Trust me. I've been here a million times," she said and patted the dock next to her. Something slapped against the water, and I decided I might prefer sitting by Abby. "Besides, if you fall through, it's only about a foot deep here."

I froze. She laughed again and started setting up her supplies.

Once I got to the end of the dock, she asked, "What was it like where you moved from?"

"Oh, I don't know. Like here, only a little bigger. Better than the last place we lived."

"How many places have you lived?" she asked.

"A few," I said and shrugged. People normally had one of two reactions when they found out how often we moved: They got extra curious and asked a whole lot of questions, or they kept their distance. I wasn't sure that I wanted either from Abby just yet.

She paused what she was doing, shaded her eyes from the sun, and looked at me. "So, I'm guessing fishing's not really your thing. What do you like to do?" she asked.

"I don't know. Movies, shopping, stuff like that." I'd learned these were things most people accepted, and it was my go-to answer concerning my interests.

Abby wrinkled up her nose but didn't say anything.

She pulled a heavy-duty purple case from her bag. It was the kind makeup artists used, with shelves of little trays that folded out to reveal more layers of shelves. If this trip was going to include makeovers, maybe I'd underestimated fishing.

"Hold this for a sec," Abby said as she handed me a plastic baggie. Instead of lip glosses or eyeshadows, it was full of plastic worms. She pulled out a tray that held hooks, rolled fishing line, a rusted pair of scissors, a pocketknife, and a box of Band-Aids.

"A long time ago, Miss Esther's husband stocked this pond. Now, it's mostly catfish and a few bluegill. But I caught a black crappie here. Hard to catch, but they're pretty. Even prettier on a plate."

"A pretty fish?" I asked.

"Fish can be pretty, if you look at them right. We're throwing them back in today, so we won't need to pull out the big guns." Abby switched to a whisper as she removed the top tray to reveal another full of little lures. Some looked like worms and lizards, some like cute versions of bugs, and others that ended in a puff of fine feathers. Her box was neat and organized—lures were sorted by type, size, and color.

"These are only for special occasions," she said as she lifted out the second tray. "This'll do for today." In the bottom of her box were two small Tupperware containers. She pulled out one and opened it.

"Is that a hot dog wiener?" I asked.

"Yep." She held it out to me.

"No, thanks. Not hungry," I said.

"Ha! Very funny." With the knife from the top tray, she cut a thin slice, then slid it on the hook. She drew her pole slowly back over her shoulder and whipped it forward as she released a button on the reel. Her line flew out across the water and landed with a soft plop near a fallen tree and some weeds.

"What's in the other container? Mustard?" I asked.

"That's the big gun, but it stinks to high heaven. Best to keep that container sealed tight," she said.

"But what is it?" I asked again.

She cut her eyes at me. "That's my dip bait. Top-secret family recipe," she whispered. "I don't mean to brag, but I'm pretty famous around here for my dip bait."

"Gram's piecrust?" I asked.

We both laughed before she shushed me. "Fish scare easy," she whispered, then bumped me gently with her shoulder.

In fourth grade, in Blessed, Alabama, I'd almost had a friend. Her name was Elizabeth. Right before Nan and I were about to move, I went over to her house. We jumped on her trampoline and I'd wanted to tell her I wouldn't be at school the next week. But I didn't. Instead, I left a papier-mâché pencil holder on her porch the day before Nan and I left. As I sat by the pond with Abby, that memory floated up and hovered over me like a swarm of gnats. Thinking of Elizabeth caused a little crack in me, an ache that was spreading, getting longer and wider like a run in a fine-gauge knit. Did having a friend make the risk of losing that friend worth it?

"Can't talk too much or we won't even get a nibble. You going to bait and cast or what?" Abby whispered again. "When I win the Family Pairs Bass Tournament, it'll take away some of the sting of not placing at Regionals. Dad and I

win almost every year. But I still need to practice my jig fishing before then."

I looked at Abby with her wild hair and
the spread of pale freckles across her nose and
cheeks. Those freckles looked like she'd been
sprinkled with something extra, and I forgot all
about pretending to know what I was doing.

"Here's the deal, Abby. I have no idea how to
bait a hook. I don't know what jig fishing is. And
I'm not all the way sure what you mean by cast,
unless you're talking about the stuff they put
over broken bones," I said.

She looked at me a second, then bumped my
shoulder with hers again and said, "Jubilee. Why
didn't you say so?"

I shrugged. "I really like to do crafts."

"Like making stuff?" she asked.

I nodded. "I love Arletta Paisley's show. She's
my idol." That was a lot of truth for me, and I felt
this tickle of excitement, like I'd shared a deep
secret.

"Oh, right, she's from here, isn't she?" Abby
asked. "I've never even seen her show."

My mouth hung open, and I almost dropped my borrowed pole in the water. "You've never watched *Queen of Neat?*" Abby shrugged and shook her head.

"She's the whole reason we moved to this town. The truth is, I thought it might make this place...I don't know. Different," I said.

A little bit of the truth was one thing, but I'd said way more than I meant to. Abby was quiet for a minute, like she knew I'd given her something private.

"I don't know about different, but I think Hope Springs is special. Best place on Earth, if you ask me," Abby said. "I'll give you a tour if you want?"

"Nan and I already drove around, but I'd like that."

"Well, not everything in Hope Springs is downtown. There's a river just east of town with a rope swing and a pretty strong current for tubing down. The trail up Ginger Hill is bright red from the clay in the dirt, and at the top, the sun lights up everything as far as you can see. Then there's Boggy Pond. Crawfish big as bananas hide under every rock. And, of course, there's the people. If I ever needed help, chances are I could ask the first person I ran into, and they'd give it."

"Giant crawfish hiding under rocks sounds terrifying, but the other stuff sounds great," I said.

Abby laughed and after a bit she asked, "Want to know a secret?"

I nodded.

"I don't just want to be a Junior Bassmaster. I want to win Nationals, and then I want to be the first woman to win the Bassmaster Classic. I didn't qualify this year, but that just means I have more time to practice for next year."

I nodded again. "Arletta says anything is possible with determination and creativity."

"That reminds me—take a look at this." She dug around in her tackle box and pulled out a lure. It was a little wooden fish painted dark green on top and light pink on bottom, with red lips and round eyes finished with cute curling eyelashes, all lacquered to a high shine. On its bottom hung two four-pronged hooks and at its tail was a sprig of thin yellow feathers. It was handcrafted, for sure.

"I made it. My grampa carves them, and I paint them. He was a pretty famous angler. People around here call him Kingfish. I'd love a nickname like that." She sighed and set the lure in my hand so I could get a closer look. "I added the eyelashes and lips. Grampa doesn't much like them. He's more of a traditionalist when it comes to lures. And most everything else."

"Now *that's* a pretty fish," I told her, handing it back. "And the eyelashes and lips are my favorite parts." She smiled and gave me her rod to hold as she baited my hook and tossed my line out across the pond from hers.

"I thought you'd like it. Listen, I'll make you a deal. I'll watch an episode of Arletta's show with you if you'll come fishing with me again. Maybe you can even bait your own hook next time."

"Deal. But you're going to have to show me more than baiting the hook if you don't want me to accidentally throw your rod into the pond," I joked.

That afternoon when I got home, the sun was shining high and hot above our new rental house. I settled on the couch, and for the first time since we got to Hope Springs, I didn't have that "wearing someone else's gym socks" feeling. And it was all because of Abby. I knew just the thing to say thank you.

ABBY'S FISH ORNAMENT

Level: Intermediate

Supplies:

* Tissue paper in at least two colors

* White printer paper, or googly eyes

* Toilet paper roll

* Twine

* Construction paper, various colors

* Small scented satchel (optional)

Tools:

* Scissors

* Double-sided tape

* Black marker

* Quarter

Directions:

1. Use a quarter to trace several circles on the tissue paper in at least two different colors (try three colors—better to be bold than boring). Use scissors to cut the circles out and then cut them in half to make semicircles for the scales.

2. Place rows of double-sided tape on the toilet paper roll, about ¼ inch apart.

3. Stick the straight edge of the semicircles to the tape, leaving the circular edge hanging off at the tail end. Alternate colors for each row and place the scales in a brick pattern. Let the circular edge of the scales overlap the previous row, so none of the toilet paper roll shows through.

4. With white paper, cut two circles to be the eyes and use the marker to draw pupils. Then, stick them on each side of the head using double-sided tape. Googly eyes would work for a less sophisticated look.

5. Place a strip of double-sided tape around inside of the roll on the tail end.

6. Cut ½-inch x 4-inch strips of tissue paper and fasten them to the tape inside the roll to form a tail.

7. Cut a piece of twine about a foot long. Thread the twine through the roll, then tie the ends together to make a big loop for hanging.

8. Use the construction paper to create personal touches, like eyelashes, beauty marks, even a bow tie. This is an opportunity to really make the craft shine and make the receiver feel it's meant just for them.

9. Optional but recommended: For a nice touch, stow a small scented satchel inside. This fish (unlike its real-life counterpart) makes for a nice room freshener and can hang from a rearview mirror, doorknob, or even a Christmas tree.

6

Blending In

Sunday afternoon, I walked down our gravel and dirt road with Abby's gift. Her house was a big two-story farmhouse with gingerbread moldings across the top of the porch. It was painted a bright yellow and the whole thing leaned a bit to the left.

Just as I was about to step onto their porch, two roaring little boys burst out of the door and ran past.

"You two better run!" A man in a cherry printed apron appeared, waving a spatula. "Oh, hello," he said. "Jubilee? Abby has been talking nonstop about you. I'm Frank: mayor's husband, cook, dinosaur wrangler, and Abby's dad. You hungry? I'm making burgers."

"I was only stopping by to give Abby something," I said.

"Come on. Best burger you'll ever eat. I swear." Abby's dad crossed his heart with the spatula and did some sort of salute. Abby walked up behind him, rolling her eyes and shaking her head.

"Hi," she said.

"Hi," I answered. "I made this for you." My arm sprang up and held out the fish ornament. I'd stuck strips of one of Nan's lavender-scented tree-shaped car deodorizers inside. Arletta always said the true crafter made do in a pinch. She did a whole segment on crafts that you can make with everyday throwaway household items. What that lady could do with the contents of a recycling bin ought to earn her a Nobel Prize.

As a rule, I did not give my creations to people face-to-face. I slid them under doors, put them on desks, even left one on the hood of a car. They were my way of saying goodbye—from a distance. But there I stood, holding out a dressed-up toilet paper roll in Abby's direction. Suddenly, my mouth went dry. "You can hang it from your doorknob in your room. Or somewhere else. If you want."

Part of me felt like throwing the stupid fish and making a run for it. But Abby hopped down the porch steps, grabbed it, and turned it slowly, a smile spreading as she noticed the freckles and eyelashes I'd glued in place one by one with Nan's tweezers.

"It has freckles!" She gave me a one-arm hug. "Thanks, Jubilee. I love it." She ran the tube under her nose and took a deep whiff. "Smells good too! You sure you don't want a burger? Dad runs the One Stop restaurant across from the stoplight in town. His burgers really are the best."

"Okay. Sure," I said and followed her inside.

The living room was covered in trucks, train tracks, and every species of toy dinosaur.

"This is what I have to live with—the twins and the wreckage they leave behind." Abby motioned to the mess and kicked a path for us. I couldn't help myself. I picked up three train tracks and half a dozen small dinosaurs and quickly tossed them in a toy box nestled under the sofa arm.

"I saw them on their way out," I said.

"And heard them too, I bet." She led me to a kitchen with a long wooden table in the center, covered with plates of sliced cheeses, tomatoes, onions, pickles, two bowls of chips, a tray stacked with toasted buns, and containers of three kinds of mustard and two that looked like mayonnaise. Nan and I didn't have that much of a spread even on Thanksgiving. And there wasn't a single marshmallow in sight.

Abby saw me staring and said, "Dad makes a big deal of Sunday lunch." Her dad walked over to the screen door leading to their backyard. He kicked it open and yelled, "Harrison! Garfield! Lunch!"

"We're all named after politicians," Abby explained. "Me after Abigail Adams, not technically a politician but close. President William Henry Harrison died after thirty-one days in office, and James Garfield made it about six months. Mom says getting really close to something big is as important as getting there. How'd you get a name like Jubilee?" she asked, grabbed a chip, chomped it, and then added, "I mean, I like it. But it's unusual."

I have a picture of my dad holding a tiny baby me and only the top of his dark head is showing because every bit of his attention is on me. Momma is in that picture and so are Wynn and Nan. They're all so young, but Nan looks just the same. Momma told me she and Daddy named me Jubilee right then and there in the delivery room because it was the happiest word they knew.

"Just something my parents thought up," I answered.

Best Christmas present Momma ever gave me was that picture and the story of how I got my name.

The twins ran in and slammed themselves into chairs. A boy with hair as yellow as canned creamed corn scooted his chair right next to mine. "My name is Garfield, and I'm already four and a half. My favorite dinosaur is a Carnotaurus because he has two horns and is a meat-eater, like me." Then he directed his teeth at my arm and chomped the air twice. Harrison had dark honey-colored hair and freckles across his nose like Abby's. He looked at me, shook his head, and rolled his eyes.

"Garfield, settle down. No biting guests." Abby's mom came in yawning and wearing a fluffy purple bathrobe that swept along the floor behind her.

"I also have some hair on my legs," Garfield whispered. Harrison nodded his head in agreement, and I laughed. Abby's family was a bit like the meal, over the top and then some.

"Me too," I whispered, and both boys smiled

and nodded as though leg hair was all it took to win them over.

"Jubilee, it's nice to finally meet you." Abby's mom held out her hand. "Myrna Standridge." She gave my hand a solid shake, and then caught herself. "Sorry, the handshaking is a bad habit, price of the job."

There was so much going on, it was hard to concentrate. Garfield thumped his sneakers against the chair legs and Harrison skitter-screeched his fork over his plate while Abby's dad whistled above a sizzling skillet and Abby's mom talked over it all. Just when I thought I might have to go outside for a deep breath, Abby leaned across and said, "Sometimes I sing 'Row, Row, Row Your Boat' in my head. Sounds weird, but it helps when things get too loud."

Nan came up with Relocation Rule Number 14: Blend in with the locals or stick out with the yokels. I wasn't even sure what a *yokel* was, but I tried blending in anyway. I noticed Abby rocking and singing with me, and we both cracked up laughing. She was right, it helped, but I wasn't sure if it was the singing or having her swaying along beside me.

"Boys, did you wash your hands?" Abby's mom asked. Both Garfield and Harrison nodded. I was certain they hadn't. Harrison looked at me and tried a wink that looked more like a series of really long blinks.

Abby's mom narrowed her eyes. "Go on and do it again. I'll supervise."

Once we all washed up, everyone loaded their plate, talked, laughed, and ate in between. And it really was the best burger I'd ever tasted.

Abby walked me out after lunch. "Thanks for the fish thingy. I have a surprise for you too. Wait here." She ran around the side of her house and came back rolling a ratty pink bike. "I know it's not much to look at. Dad used to call it my 'big girl' bike, but I got a BMX for Christmas. So, I thought, since you like making things, maybe you could fix it up and use it. Then we could ride all over town together."

"Thanks, Abby. I love it," I said. I wasn't sure I could ride it. I wasn't sure Arletta herself could glamorganize the dingy out of that two-wheeler, but I did love it.

Abby gave me a quick hug goodbye before I rolled the bike down their driveway and waved back at her. That sun-faded, rust-spattered bike was the ugliest, most perfect thing anyone had ever given me.

Though I was full of food, I felt emptied out too. Spending time with families, even seeing big families in SmartMart or stuffed in a mini-van, sometimes did that to me. Nan and I were a family, and we were happy. But we weren't busting at the seams with it.

I steered my new-old bike down the dirt road in a daze, which is maybe why I didn't notice the ambulance pulled up in our driveway until I was standing beside it.

Globsnotting Pink Curtains

N an!" I dropped the bike and ran to the door. "Nan!"

A woman in a uniform blocked the doorway. "Everything is fine. Your grandma fell, but she's okay."

I looked past the woman's shoulder. A man in a matching uniform leaned over a sprawled-out and groaning lump on the floor wearing Nan's high-heeled clogs. "Nan!" I yelled over my thundering heart.

The woman lowered a hand onto my shoulder.

"She's fine. Worst case, she's got some broken bones. My partner is checking her out, and then we'll take her down to the hospital for some X-rays. You know anyone named Pink?"

"What?" I asked. "No." My voice was shaky and high, squeezed tight by the worry filling up my whole body.

"Well, she keeps saying that this is all Pink's fault," she said. "You can go talk to her before we transport her. Got anyone you can call?"

Rather than say no, I rushed past her and fell to my knees next to Nan.

"Nan, are you okay? I'm sorry. I shouldn't have left you alone here with all this work to do." Tears rolled down my face and I quickly wiped them off.

"It's not your fault. It's my own and those dognasty, globsnotting PINK curtains!" Nan yelled and motioned to a toppled chair and a pile of pink fabric, winced, and grabbed her ribs. "I couldn't stand them another second. I fell off the chair and cracked my side on the coffee table and twisted my ankle on the way down."

"Ma'am, relax and be still," the male paramedic said, pressing a hand on Nan's arm.

She shrugged his hand off. "I'm a nurse. I'm due to start work at the nursing home tomorrow. Sorry I even called. Just a few bruised ribs, and I knocked my wind out. You guys can go on and get, and thank you very much."

"Ma'am, we still need to take you in, and besides, you won't be able to start work on Monday, not on that ankle. It's already swelling, and your ribs need a closer look too," he said. He shook his head, then tried to sneak a glance at the other EMT, but Nan caught him.

"My name is Nan Johnson, not ma'am. My call was an overreaction. I'm fine. Right as rain." She sounded firm, tried to stand, and then cried out in pain. The paramedic helped her to the couch. Nan sucked in short breaths, and I noticed her ankle was already puffy, swelling so much the bone hardly seemed to be there at all. My muscles, my heart, and everything else inside clenched up, like they all jumped and huddled together for support.

"Just relax, Mrs. Johnson. We'll get you in the ambulance and have X-rays done in no time," the female paramedic said. "You're going to be working at the nursing home?"

"That's right," Nan answered.

"And this is Dr. Burgess's rental house? He's doing rounds at the hospital now. This is his mother's house you're renting. Why don't we let the doctor check you out? Just to be safe. So your granddaughter here won't worry," she said.

I nodded at Nan. "I'll go with you," I said, but my voice was all sobby and choked, so I cleared my throat and said it again. "I'll go with you, Nan."

"Sure, she can ride along in the ambulance. No problem," the female paramedic said.

"All right. Fine," Nan said, giving up. "Jubilee, grab my bag and my phone, will you?"

In the ambulance, machines beeped and whirred. Nan wasn't hooked up to any of them, but even so, after a while it felt like each beep was talking to me.

BEEP: Spending time with another family.

BEEP: You were gone too long.

BEEP: This never would have happened if you'd been there.

BEEP: What will you do without Nan?

I held Nan's hand and rested my forehead on the edge of the gurney. What would I do without her? The thought froze me solid. I couldn't even imagine it. It was warm, even with the air-conditioning roaring, but I felt like I might break into a fit of shakes. Momma! Momma didn't even know we'd moved!

I cried and didn't bother to wipe away the evidence. Though Nan was the one who was hurt, she kept whispering to me, "It'll be okay." By the time we got to the hospital, I could barely hold my head up.

They made Nan lie on a stretcher and wheeled her in while she yelled, "This is completely unnecessary!" three or four times and said more almost-curses than I could count—a few full-on real curses too.

I followed her down a short hallway. All I

could manage was a whispered, "I'll be right here, Nan."

They wheeled her off for X-rays, and the female paramedic showed me where to wait. She nudged my shoulder. "She's only banged up. She'll be fine." Then she whispered, "She's right, though. A lot of it is unnecessary. But better to be safe."

I kept my head down.

"You want a Coke?"

I shrugged, and minutes later she handed me a cold can of soda. It was so quiet in the hallway, I could hear the bubbles fizzing inside the can.

Some nurses laughed at the front desk, and I shot them a look. Because of Nan's jobs, I'd seen as many hospitals as I had new schools. One of the nurses smiled, came around the desk, and walked toward me. I stared at her shoes, wishing that when I looked up, it'd be Nan standing there, right as rain just like she'd said. "Hey, sweetheart, you want to use our phone to call someone? Might be nice to have some company while you wait?"

I looked up, shook my head, and said, "No, thank you."

I sat in a plastic chair, staring at a row of identical seats across from me, each with at least one rusty leg. Paintings lined the hallway, all calm country scenes. Cows and pastures, tractors and grain silos. The painting right in front of me showed five geese flying over a red barn. But they weren't relaxing me any. My pulse and my mind were racing. If Nan was really hurt, we'd need Momma's help. I couldn't call her without a plan—a plan and a really good excuse for not contacting her sooner.

Recently, Momma'd made a fuss about our relocating, and that fuss got louder and turned into an almost-argument after our last move. I didn't want to give Momma any extra reasons to cause trouble.

The doctor came over to where I was waiting, leaned over, and spoke to me with his face so close to mine I could smell his minty breath. "I'm Dr. Burgess. Your grandmother is going to be fine. She's got a fractured rib and a hairline fracture in her ankle. The good news is, the breaks aren't bad. She'll need a wrap on her ribs and an Aircast on the ankle." I started to cry again.

Dr. Burgess pulled a folded tissue from his pocket. "It sounds like a lot, but they're all minor injuries. She'll be fine if she takes it easy. You guys are living in Mother's old house, so I know there are no stairs, but Nan will need more help than usual. She can't drive. Is there anyone to help you?"

If I said no, then that might turn all my problems from regular-sized to Texas-sized. If I said yes, then I'd have to call Momma. Even if it was for a week or two, I didn't want to ask if I could stay with her. She was on tour, and asking for help now meant she'd have to give that up—or that she wouldn't. I'd rather not ask than deal with the answer. And without me, what would Nan do? So I said, "Yes, I've already talked to my mom."

I didn't normally tell through-and-through lies. Nan had a stockpile of quotes about lying, but I knew the situation called for more fibbing than usual, at least until I'd worked out what to do next.

Dr. Burgess smiled at me. "I hear Nan did battle with Mother's old curtains." He laughed. "I can't count how many times I wanted to tear those things down myself. But considering Nan's current condition, no more renovations without doctor and landlord approval. All right?"

I nodded.

He said Nan needed help, but he didn't say that help couldn't be from me. Nan and I, we stuck together. Sure, normally she was helping me, but I could manage the other way around. I just had to figure out how. When we were short on money—which happened a lot—we had to get creative with what we had and make it count, as per Relocation Rule Number 17: Forget what's missing, and work with what's not. That's what I needed to do now.

It dawned on me that I had more to work with than usual. To start with, I had Abby's number, and I had Nan's cell phone. Nan wouldn't like it, but it was going to take more than just the two of us. I'd prefer that excluded Momma for as long as possible.

When I walked into Nan's room, she looked like my regular old Nan, only a little rumpled. "Jubilee," she said and grimaced as she stood. "Lord, if it didn't hurt to breathe, I'd hug you and never let go." She reached out, cupped my chin, and raised my face so I looked her in the eyes. "You don't have a thing to feel bad about. It was an accident, and my fault." She switched to a whisper. "Now, let's get the heck out of this dump."

Abby and her mother picked us up in their beat-up minivan. I held Nan's crutches as Abby's mom tried to help her in, but Nan grunted, gritted her teeth, and got into the van on her own.

After a quick introduction, Abby's mom talked and talked, and I was glad for the distraction. "Don't worry, Nan. I've already got you signed up for A-Meal-to-Heal. A bunch of local churches work with all the restaurants in town and deliver to anyone homebound and healing. So, that's you for the next few weeks. Normally, they stop and visit for a while too. Frank, that's my husband, his restaurant, the One Stop, participates. And Abby's going to ride her bike down every afternoon to check in. Don't bother protesting. I'm the mayor. I get my way." Abby's mom smiled, but I could tell she meant business.

I began to feel like things might be all right, that I might be able to handle it. Abby squeezed my hand and smiled at me. I felt myself smile back and leak another tear. The only person not smiling was Nan. She prided herself on not needing any help, and I guessed needing some now bothered her almost as much as the pain.

As soon as their minivan spewed dust on its way out of our driveway, Nan hobbled to our door. She muttered, "Home sweet home," before going in, her voice thick with sarcasm.

I stood in our new yard, not brown now but lit gray-blue from the full moon, and I listened to the nighttime chorus of singing toads and bugs. Even though I knew they couldn't see me, I waved as Abby's van turned toward her house and watched until I couldn't see their taillights.

Abby's mom worked out all but one of my problems in a single ten-minute car ride. No wonder she was the mayor.

Momma's check went toward our rent, and Nan's money went to everything else. I eyed the shed behind our rental house and was reminded of one of the paintings at the hospital, the red barn. I had an idea. Maybe if I could sort out the everything else, I could worry about Momma later.

The moon hung low over a ridge lined with pines and oak trees. I almost whispered what Nan had said, only without the sarcasm. Instead, I closed my eyes, and thought those three words— *home sweet home*—more like a wish or prayer, and went inside.

8

Arlene Peavey

When it came to Abby, I didn't have much of a choice whether to like her. I just did. And now, I didn't have much choice about whether to depend on her. Monday morning, she showed up carrying a box loaded to the top with two loaves of banana bread, two pies, peanut butter cookies, corn muffins, a dish of macaroni and cheese, and a lasagna. "From Dad. He went a little overboard," she said.

I waved her in and took the box to the kitchen

table. "The A-Meal-to-Heal people should come soon. My errand might take an hour or so," I said.

"Sure. What's the errand?" Abby asked.

"Just to town." I'd already asked Nan if I could ride to town and she'd agreed. Abby nodded and didn't ask for more details.

"I don't need a babysitter," Nan argued. She'd let me fix her hair and help her get dressed. If I ignored the limp and the wincing with every other movement, she looked great.

"Nan, you might need to reach something or pick something up. You need help. That's why Abby's here," I said. Abby nodded.

"And I appreciate it," Nan said. That was as close to an agreement as I was going to get.

"I just want to watch some non-twin TV. Can't take another minute of singing adults dressed like birds and beavers," Abby said. We made a plan for the whole afternoon, and her dad was ready, should Nan need anything big. But if Nan found out I'd asked for even more help, she might break her other ankle pitching a fit.

My new-old bike turned out to be more than hard on the eyes. Abby must have been a foot shorter the last time she rode it. I couldn't figure out how to raise the seat, so my knees almost touched my earlobes when I pedaled. To make matters worse, I had dressed for success, not a bike ride. My skirt rose with every pedal push, and I almost wrecked three times trying to hold it down and steer one-handed.

My reflection in the window of the Fabric Barn was almost enough to keep me from going in. The clothes I'd spent so much time picking out were wrinkled and covered in dust, and strands of my hair had escaped my ponytail and curled out in a thin frizz halo. But I was willing to sacrifice my dignity if it meant I got to keep holding on to Hope Springs and my dream of the perfect place for me and Nan.

Both Holly Paine and Rayburn were almost exactly as Nan and I first found them. Only this time, instead of a book, Holly was reading the *Hope Springs Gazette* with Rayburn snoring at her feet.

I stood in front of her for a full minute before

she folded the paper in half. "Almost done," she muttered. Then she smacked it down on the counter and said, "That SmartMart outside of town is going to be open twenty-four hours a day, seven days a week. A Supercenter is what they're calling it." She scanned me over. "Honey, you look a mess."

"I love to shop at SmartMart," I said, deciding to ignore the other comment.

"That's the problem. Everybody loves to shop there. All the local businesses will get shut out." She slid the paper into the trash can. "Oh well, not much I can do. But maybe I can do something for you. I heard about Nan's fall."

"I came to take you up on the job offer. I could start today." I felt good for two reasons. One: I was being what Nan called "proactive," taking charge and doing something. Two: The new season of *Queen of Neat* premiered in a few short hours, and Abby was staying to watch it with me. A sort of constant tremble rattled around my insides, like my nervousness and excitement were being mixed on high.

"Well, sure. I've needed help getting this place in order for years. Might as well start today. How about you help me sort out my back storage room? I'll pay you at the end of the week. That sound good?" she asked.

I nodded. Surely, Nan and I could make do until the end of the week. We had plenty of food, and even if we needed gas money, Nan wouldn't be driving anywhere.

Holly brushed her hands on her jeans and stood. "Follow me." She led me to a door behind the counter. Rayburn readjusted his back end and panted from the effort. "I've got all the new orders in here. Problem is, I've got no place to put them."

The back room was more of a tangled mess than the front. Unopened boxes were stacked along one wall, and bolts of fabric lay piled in tall pyramids covering almost every inch of floor space. The chaos left me speechless.

"I know. It's bad," Holly said.

Only a small space was free of any clutter. Standing in the clearing was something that looked like a table but, instead of a slab on top, it had only the edges, like old fancy table legs supporting a big empty picture frame. "What's that?" I asked. I noticed the top part was more complicated than I'd thought. It wasn't just a frame, but had aligned moving pieces and what looked like gears with little levers attached to the sides.

"A quilting frame. I used to have classes here. You ever work on quilts?" Holly ran her palm over the smooth wooden edge of the frame. "One of the oldest crafts there is, one with real heart. I could teach you, if you want?"

Right then, my skin was too busy crawling and my fingers too busy itching to organize to answer. I couldn't think of anything but cleaning up. "Some of this is brand new," I said.

"More than some. I couldn't find any space for it."

"What about moving everything that's really old to a sale rack at the back? And put the newest stuff up front. That way, people have to walk by the new bolts to get to the sale rack. Maybe they'll see something they like on both," I said. I switched to a whisper. "And the really, really old stuff, we could advertise as vintage and charge twice as much."

"I'm impressed. You've earned your first bonus. Two yards of any fabric you like, on the house." She patted me on the back. I smiled but thought, if Holly gave things away so easily, she'd run herself out of business before SmartMart did.

While we worked, a customer came in and Holly cut her two yards of pale green flannel. I noticed, when the woman paid, she took out a stack of fabric scraps and said, "For your collection." Holly took the scraps and put them in a five-gallon bucket behind the counter.

I covered an old sign with a yard of rough linen and then used rickrack, buttons, old zippers, and fabric tape to spell out SALE. All Holly had was a bottle of age-thickened Elmer's glue, so the corners were sloppy. But Holly was impressed again. "I swear you've got a natural knack for this stuff."

"Everything I know I learned from Hope Springs's own Arletta Paisley," I said.

Holly froze, looking like she'd swallowed a pincushion.

"Is that so?" she asked.

"Yes, did you know her when she lived here?" I asked. I'd wanted to ask her about Arletta since the first time Nan and I walked in her store.

"I did," Holly said, and went back to work.

I waited. Nothing.

"Did you know her well?" I asked.

"I knew her well enough. We even had a few classes together in high school. Back then, she was a brunette and her name was Arlene Peavey. She was only here for senior year and, as far as I know, hasn't been back since." She looked at me and sighed. "I'm sorry, honey, but my guess is that her reminiscing on air about Hope Springs is as genuine as her hair color."

It was like she'd snatched something right out of my hands, and it took me some time for the shock to wear off. "Well, I bet there's not a single person in showbiz with their true hair color," I pointed out.

"Ha! I bet you're right about that." Holly laughed and went back to sorting her scraps.

But I couldn't shrug off what she'd said. What was it with the people in this town? First, Abby'd never even seen the show, and now Holly had practically called Arletta a fake.

After that, I didn't have a whole lot to say to Holly Paine. I knew from experience she was holding something back. The longer I worked, the more my anger bubbled until it reached a steady simmer. I didn't want to hear any more of what she thought anyway. Fine by me. Who was Holly Paine to me, really? I hardly knew her.

I smoothed my skirt with both hands and got back to work. For an hour, I moved bolts of fabric, slammed them into place, huffed through my nostrils like a charging bull, and kept my mouth shut. The rosemary citrus room freshener I'd made for Holly sat in my backpack, and I decided to leave it right where it was.

The first time I had watched *Queen of Neat*,

Nan and I had just started our nine-month stay in Bigheart, Oklahoma. It'd been another first day, but one that hurt worse than all the others because I missed having a friend. I decided then and there it wasn't worth making another one.

I had no momma to snuggle up to and tell my problems. Nan had never been one to cuddle, and her way of dealing with problems was to move. So I curled up on the couch and turned on the TV. And there was Arletta Paisley—her rounded cheeks lifted by an easy smile, blonde, with deep blue eyes, all soft and comforting. She was almost exactly the snuggling kind of momma I'd been picturing.

The more I thought about what Holly'd said, the madder I got, until that simmer reached a rolling boil. What would Holly Paine know about hair dye with that long gray braid? I carried an armload of fabric bolts and a mouth full of unspoken sass when the front door swung open and in walked a boy with shaggy brown hair poking out from under a Texas Rangers baseball cap—the same boy that watched me not make a wish. The sight forced thoughts of Holly and Arletta Paisley right out of my mind, distracting me enough that I tripped over the pile of velvet bolts I was sorting and fell face-first into a hanging rack of upholstery-grade damask.

"Umm, Jubilee, this is my nephew, Colton Griggs. He works at the hardware store," Holly said in my direction. I was pretty sure I'd knocked my ponytail crooked.

"Nice to meet you," I managed. I stood, tried to straighten my hair, and smiled. Was this the same Colton who usually fished with Abby? I guessed there couldn't be more than one in a town this small. "Abby mentioned you," I added.

"Yeah," he said. I couldn't tell if his answer was a question or a statement. I would've thought he was a total weirdo if he hadn't smiled. That smile erased most of my negative thoughts.

Colton handed Holly a paper bag, turned, and left without another word.

"Colton's dad, my little brother, owns Hope Springs Hardware and Griggs' Rigs Racing. Hardware store is two doors down. The racetrack is south of town and just shy of insanity if you ask me," Holly said. "Thought you could use this." She handed me the bag. Inside was a heavy-duty glue gun. "For your next project."

I managed a weak thank-you. Maybe Holly had some wrongheaded ideas about Arletta, but if she knew when a glue gun was in order, she wasn't all bad.

Holly tuned the radio to a country station, and we worked. I knew I needed to get back to Nan but didn't feel like I could take a gift and run. A lively song came on, Holly shimmied, and I squeezed out a smile.

When another customer came in and gave her a bundle of scrap fabric, I couldn't resist asking.

"Why did she give you her garbage?" I asked.

"Those are remnants, honey, not garbage. There's a big difference. I use them in my quilts. This," she said, and pulled out a scrap of a cotton Liberty print of lilac rose buds, "is from the dress she made her granddaughter. And these," she continued, holding up another bundle, "are from the lap quilt she made for her mother.

These are little snippets of people's lives. I'd love to teach you to quilt. You'd be a natural."

"Thanks," I said. Holly'd been nothing but generous. If I expected Nan to give second chances, then I could start by doing it myself.

I'd accidentally stayed almost two hours. Before I grabbed my backpack from behind the counter, I went ahead and left the mason jar of air freshener. I noticed the newspaper draped over the edge of the wastebasket and pulled it out.

"I better get back to Nan." I held up the paper. "Mind if I take this?"

Holly only nodded and went back to looking through her fabric scraps. "Sure. See you soon."

As I stepped out the door, I thought I heard Momma's warbled voice float up out of Holly's old radio. There was no mistaking that tone—it was Momma for sure. Getting radio time was a big deal, one she hadn't even bothered to tell me about.

With each pump of the pedals, I gritted my teeth and tried pushing Momma out of my head.

I tried, but it wasn't working. With dust and my own knees flying in my face, and Momma's voice ringing around in my head, I pedaled so hard and fast that I was panting worse than poor Rayburn by the time I turned down our road.

9

Good Luck and Wishes Come True

A blush-pink Cadillac stuck out from behind Nan's dusty car. I let my bike fall in the yard. Either something else had happened, or old Mrs. Burgess had come back from the dead to curse Nan for tearing down her curtains. I ran up our drive and only relaxed when I saw A-Meal-to-Heal sticker on the back window.

Abby sat with Nan at the kitchen table while a lady old enough to be personal friends with Betsy Ross, sewer of the first US flag, hobbled around the kitchen. Nan didn't look pleased, and

I guessed I didn't either. Abby gave me an apologetic look and shrugged. With only fifteen minutes and counting until Arletta Paisley's new show, I didn't have time for chitchat.

The lady turned to me and said, "Well, you ought to be ashamed of yourself. Leaving your poor grandmother while you hang around that Holly Paine learning goodness knows what." She turned her head to Nan and said in a loud whisper, "That woman reads nothing but trash."

I plastered on a smile pretty as a string of pearls. "Hello, nice to meet you. I'm Jubilee, and you are?" Relocation Rule Number 5: Nothing takes the air out of a tense situation like extreme politeness and a big smile.

But this lady wasn't fooled. She put one hand on the hip of her polyester slacks and took a few steps forward. "I'm Esther Gibbons. Everyone in this town calls me Miss Esther. I believe you've already met my pond?" She motioned to Abby. "Abby's a good girl, so at least you've got that going for you."

"Miss Esther, I really appreciate the casseroles

you brought over." Nan paused. "And the company. Of course. But really, I'm fine, and I gave Jubilee permission to leave. Like I told you, she's working at the Fabric Barn. We feel it's important to get involved in the community right away." She winked at me behind Miss Esther's back. I saw it, but so did Abby. "I really don't know what I'd do if it weren't for all the kindness you folks have shown me and Jubilee. 'Kindness is the language the deaf can hear and the blind can see.' Mark—"

"Yes, yes, I know. Mark Twain," Miss Esther interrupted. "A real smart aleck, if you ask me. I was the school librarian for almost forty years. Mrs. Burgess was a good woman and my best friend. I consider it my personal responsibility to make sure the people staying in this house are treated well." She turned to me. "Listen here. I'm coming back tomorrow afternoon, and I want a full report on who's coming by and if there's anyone else who can help out. Nan Johnson, you're going to be on the mend for a few weeks." With that, she hobbled to the door, but before leaving, she turned, pointed two fingers at her eyes, and then pointed them at me.

I smiled and slammed the door shut.

"No wonder this house was empty," I said as soon as the door closed.

Abby laughed. "Miss Esther is okay. She does come off a bit strong sometimes."

"'Every man is surrounded by a neighborhood of voluntary spies.' Jane Austen." Nan grimaced as she stood. Abby furrowed her brow and looked at me, but I just shook my head.

"Are you all right?" I asked, even though I knew she wasn't. Nan didn't grimace; she smiled and then changed the topic. "Sorry I'm so late," I added.

Other than SmartMart, Nan was my one and only thing that stayed the same. Seeing her so changed made me feel as if I stood on a fault line and any moment my whole life might crack apart. I looked over at Abby again. She began straightening up the kitchen, putting away the leftovers and piling dishes in the sink. It was like she read my mind, and I felt sorry for it because, for a split second, I'd wished she wasn't there.

"Why don't you go lie down?" I asked.

"All right. I think I will. I know you two are excited about your show. There are about fifteen frozen casseroles in the freezer for dinner. Turn the oven to... Doggone it, I already forgot. Probably could just stick it in the microwave." Abby shook her head behind Nan's back.

I followed Nan into the living room. "Everything's going to be all right," I whispered, more to myself than to Nan.

"Sure, it is. I'll be better in no time," she said. "Enjoy your show." She switched to a whisper. "Abby's a real find. I like her." Then she shuffled down the hall.

I turned to Abby. "You ready?"

She shrugged. "Sure. But whatever you do, don't put a frozen casserole in the microwave."

"Just a minute." I rushed to my room and grabbed my notebook plus a blank one for Abby. I also took three bunches of sticky notes, my whole bundle of sharpened pencils, a few pens, and ran back to the living room.

Abby came over and sat on the couch while I quickly organized our supplies into piles. "What's all this for?" she asked.

I handed her the blank notebook. "For notes, of course."

"For notes," she repeated and nodded. "Of course."

I flipped the TV on just as Arletta Paisley's intro started up. They hadn't changed a thing—same scenes from old episodes, same light country music. I took a deep breath and sank down into the cushions. Now, this was more like it; this I could count on.

Then Arletta Paisley's grinning face filled the screen. But instead of sitting on her beat-up oak stool next to the marble countertop of her kitchen island or standing behind her weathered wood crafting table, her white walls accented with aqua and lemony yellow knickknacks, she was perched on an overstuffed leather sofa in front of a live studio audience. Behind her was the largest flat screen on the planet flashing stills from previous shows. I watched slack-jawed with shock.

"This isn't right," I whispered.

"What's not right?" Abby asked. I didn't have the time or the words to answer.

Arletta Paisley gave her extra-big smile to the camera. I relaxed a little. "Well, I'm so glad y'all could join me for a brand-new season of *Queen of Neat*," she said to an eruption of clapping and hollering from the live audience. Live!

"We're trying something a little new this season. Along with our wonderful sponsors at Smart-Mart, we're traveling around to America's small towns, glamorganizing as we go." She paused and winked, then laughed and clapped through another burst of audience noise. "We're hoping to get out there, get to the heart and soul of this great country, and really show how crafting can touch lives. And this is particularly special to me, because this season we'll be filming an episode in my sweet hometown of Hope Springs, Texas." She clutched her chest and even looked a little teary.

I dropped my pencil. Then I grabbed a pillow from the couch and screamed into it loud enough for old Mrs. Burgess to hear, rest her soul.

I looked at Abby. "Arletta Paisley is coming to Hope Springs!" I yelled.

"So I've heard." She laughed and picked up her pencil. "But I'll write it down so I don't forget." I bumped her on the shoulder and grinned as she jotted it in bold all caps.

The episode featured little crafts that beginners could do to "bring some light" to people in hospitals or nursing homes. Arletta invited a nurse, a doctor, and one ninety-five-year-old lady in an oxygen mask onto the stage, and they crafted and chatted behind a big white table. She described the season's ongoing theme as "charitable crafts" because "it's not just our own lives that get messy." Before signing off, she mentioned that SmartMart provided all the materials for the crafts, which was met with another explosion of applause and then straight to commercial.

For the first time, I didn't take a single note. I sat on the couch after the show, my pencil still poised over a blank page, and stared straight ahead. Arletta Paisley was coming to Hope Springs. ARLETTA PAISLEY WAS COMING TO HOPE SPRINGS!!!! I felt like I'd been wrapped in silk tulle made of good luck and wishes come true.

Abby nudged me. "You all right?"

"I'm good. Wait. I'm better than good. I'm fantastic!"

She laughed and shook her head. "I'd better go. If I'm ten minutes late, Mom will call Sheriff Whitaker."

I walked her to the door and watched until she reached the end of our drive.

"Hey, guess what?" I yelled.

She stopped and turned around. "Umm. Is it that Arletta Paisley is coming here?"

"YES!" I howled.

Abby laughed. "Do me a favor and maybe don't eat so many marshmallows?"

She walked backward a few steps and waved, and I waved back. I might have hopped up and down a little too.

As I shut the door and turned toward the kitchen, Nan's cell phone caught my eye from where it rested next to my backpack on the kitchen table. I remembered the newspaper I'd slipped out of Holly's trash. But I also remembered Momma's voice floating out of the radio. I'd have to talk to her sooner or later. But for now, I was choosing later. I took the newspaper, settled back on the couch, and found the article.

Besides, Momma never made Nan anything but worse.

SMARTMART: OPPORTUNITY OR THREAT?

Chances are, if you stop a stranger on the street in Hope Springs, they'll have an opinion about the SmartMart Superstore on I-230 south of town. The store is on schedule to open at the end of the summer. As the opening draws near, apprehensions of small business owners rise, while others welcome the employment opportunities and shopping conveniences a SmartMart promises.

With the signing of Hope Springs's own

Arletta Paisley as the face of SmartMart, people seem to be even more divided. As well as a nationally recognizable face, Paisley brings the power of her Hearth & Home Network show, *Queen of Neat*. Each episode has been reformatted to promote the SmartMart brand.

A Hope Springs business owner was quoted as saying, "I can't compete with Smart-Mart prices because they buy in bulk from outside the US. But people don't care so much about buying local if SmartMart has what they want and it's cheaper." In contrast, another resident complained of the local employment opportunities and lack of shopping choices. "There are lots of things that are hard to find around here, including jobs. The way I see it, SmartMart solves both those problems."

One thing is clear: If SmartMart prices can't be beat, as the mega-chain claims, local shops are in trouble. But cheaper merchandise isn't always better, leaving local entrepreneurs to prove that quality is queen.

10

Having It Wrong

I woke the next morning with a blurred image of my momma left over from some dream I couldn't remember. Since I'd heard her singing voice, Momma'd been sneaking her way into my mind. Maybe it was that I'd let Nan think I'd called her, or maybe it was that she hadn't called me back—or called at all in months.

When I shuffled into the hallway, I heard Nan on the phone. She saw me and switched to a whisper. "Yes, I understand. I'll get the payment to you as soon as I can."

Nan shut off her phone and smiled at me. "Electric company. The account is under Dr. Burgess's name, and we need to switch it over. They want a deposit."

Before moving to Hope Springs, the idea of Arletta Paisley within spitting distance would've caused me to fly into a million pieces. And for one full evening, I flat-out soared. Then I remembered everything else and hit the ground hard.

Nan limped over to the couch. Her hair was flat on one side, and she wore the same clothes I'd helped her into the day before. She slowly lowered herself onto the cushions, sucking air through her teeth in short bursts until she sat next to me.

"Feeling bad today?" I asked.

She shook her head, but there was no doubt about it. She was lying.

"I'll help you get dressed again," I offered. She patted my knee, and I could tell that even slight movement hurt her ribs.

"I'll call and see what I can do about getting some stronger pain medication. And then we'll have to figure out a way to go pick it up," she said.

Deposits were normally a few hundred dollars, and who knew how much medication would cost. I wasn't going to earn enough money at the Fabric Barn to make a real difference, and I couldn't take care of Nan on my own. We were a team, but like one of Abby's baited hooks, we were sinking fast.

"Nan, I know it's normally just the two of us. But what if this time we let some people help. I barely know Abby, but you said yourself she's great. There's Holly too." I wanted to say more, but I could feel Nan straighten next to me.

"I'll figure something out," Nan said. "I've always taken care of us, haven't I?"

I nodded. She narrowed her eyes and asked, "Is there something else going on?"

I normally didn't keep secrets.

"Nan, I haven't talked to Momma," I said.

"Oh, I'll call her. I should've called her right after I fell," she said.

I looked at her and then down at the floor.

"You mean, you never called her? At all?"

I kept my eyes down. "I called. She just never called back. And then I didn't call again. I don't know...I was mad at her, I guess."

Nan took a deep breath and winced. Then we both stared at her phone.

"Well, we don't need her permission to move. But I should've at least let her know. She's going to be hopping mad, that's for sure." She picked up the phone. "'A man can be destroyed but not defeated,'" she said.

"Hemingway again?" I asked. Nan nodded.

I always thought of Nan as tough as beef jerky. This talk of being destroyed reminded me more of marshmallows—squashed ones.

"Don't worry. We all make mistakes. I'll sort it out with your momma. She should understand making mistakes well enough."

Nan dialed, and I crossed my arms, held tight, and listened in. Momma answered, and as soon as Nan told her we'd moved, things headed south fast. "What's best for Jubilee? You gave up the right to make that decision a long time ago,"

Nan said. Then I couldn't make out what exactly Momma said after that, only that she had a lot to say, and she said it loudly. Nan interrupted occasionally and said, "I know. I should've called sooner." Then Nan told her about being injured. She waited a bit before holding the phone out to me. "She wants to talk to you."

If I could've said no, I would've.

I called Momma on her birthday, and she called me on mine. She and Wynn came at Christmas and stayed a few hours. Nan and Wynn got along, but those hours were full of tightness and a lot of quiet. Wynn did most of the talking.

"Jubi, honey, I'm so glad Nan called. I was just thinking about you." Momma's voice was light and soft, welcoming almost, like her singing voice.

"Hi, Momma."

Well, at least this time I had something to say to her. I told her the move was my idea, I told her that I'd let Nan think I'd called, and I told her that I left a message with Wynn. I thought I'd smoothed everything out, that maybe it wasn't so bad after all. But then the unthinkable: "I'll be there no later than five," she said. "I promise." She ended the call without a goodbye.

Nan patted my leg. "I'm sorry I lost my temper. You shouldn't have to hear me and your momma argue."

"She's coming," I said.

"Today?" Nan asked. I nodded. "Well, we better get dressed and straighten up," she said. "But let's not hold our breath." She gave my hand a squeeze. Just like Nan never met a town she couldn't bear to part with, Momma never made a promise she wasn't willing to break.

So, late that afternoon, I sat on the porch and waited. I was experienced in waiting for Momma. Despite Nan's warning, I was excited and nervous, but after fidgeting for over an hour that nervousness developed a sour edge. Once, in kindergarten, Momma forgot to come get me—just completely forgot all about me. I sat in the office while the school secretary sighed and looked at the clock. My teacher called Nan, and when she got there, they spoke in the hallway in whispers.

Not long after that, I moved in with Nan, and not too long after that, Nan and I moved for the first time.

Wynn's truck pulled into our driveway around seven o'clock that evening, long after I'd given up and gone inside. Momma stepped out of the truck with dusk as a backdrop. She wore skinny jeans and a long white gauzy shirt cinched around her tiny waist with a wide leather belt. Her hair blew around, and a pair of huge sunglasses hid most of her face. She looked like a movie star or a genuine country music singer, not the Momma I'd last seen nearly six months ago.

Nan said Daddy'd stayed behind to take care of me when Momma got her first touring gig. And again on her second. One night they'd had a big argument about her never being around. He left on the motorcycle and never came back. Nan said it wasn't anyone's fault, but I could tell she didn't believe it. What she didn't say was that Momma dumped me after my daddy died because it was easier—easier to fall to pieces without me to worry about. And easier for her to get better and move on with her dream once I was out of the way.

Her letters can't change the truth.

Momma rushed over and wrapped her arms around me. She smelled like roses, sweet and sharp.

"Jubi, you look beautiful," she said and touched one of my dark curls. I saw parts of my face in hers.

Just looking at her hurt a little.

Wynn wiped the dust off his black boots with his hands and then tried to clap the dirt off. The boots had a white panel with little red roses stitched into the leather. Even his footwear was too much. He gave me a wide smile and lifted me off the ground with a hug. "Let's see that grandma of yours," he said. He put me down and whispered, "Don't worry." And those two words, combined with the way Momma stomped toward the front door, made me worry a million times more.

Nan was sitting on the couch when we walked

in. She'd done her best to get ready, but she sure didn't look up for a fight.

"Nan, how are you?" Momma asked. They never quite looked each other in the eyes. Mostly, they picked something to stare at and then talked. Nan chose a spot on the ceiling, and Momma gazed off in the direction of the kitchen.

"Been better," Nan said. "But, Alexandra, I'll be fine in a few weeks. In fact, this all seems a little extreme to me."

"Nan, no one's as tough as you. Believe me, I know that better than most," Momma said, and her voice made it clear she didn't mean it as a compliment. "But someone's got to be around to help out, get the groceries, drive Jubi to register for school, make dinners. Maybe provide a little stability in the wake of all this?"

I knew the look on Nan's face. It was the get-out-the-maps look. She stood, cleared her throat to cover the little whimper she made whenever she got off the couch, and said, "I'll let you visit with Jubilee while I go freshen up for dinner." She wasn't hitting the road, but she was making a run for it. She looked at Wynn. "Nice to see you again." Then she glared at Momma, making a point of leaving her out, and hobbled down the hallway.

"That went well," Wynn said as soon as Nan's door closed.

Momma gave me a sad smile and shrugged. She looked around at our rental house and said, "This is a nice one you two picked out. I like the curtains." She pointed to the pink ones Nan hadn't managed to rip down. "Well, show us around. Let's see how you're living."

There wasn't much to show. But as I opened the door to my craft room, I felt a rush of pride. I'd done everything in there myself.

"Wow, Jubi," Wynn said. "Your own hobby room." Hobby! I clenched my hands into fists, but Wynn caught his mistake. "I mean, it's a beautiful craft room. Looks fit to be filmed." Wynn knew I loved Arletta Paisley, and he occasionally sent me gifts from Arletta's housewares line. Momma signed the cards, but I knew they were from Wynn. Last Christmas, he couldn't keep himself from asking if I'd liked the desk organizer Momma sent. I loved him. But love is tricky. Sometimes, I couldn't help remembering he was Momma's number one ally, that she stuck with him and not with me. Or maybe it was the other way around, and what bothered me was that he stuck with her after she'd given me up.

"It's nice, real nice," Momma said. She put her hand on my arm, and I thought of us as clashing prints, like orange paisley satin and red checked gingham. No way to put those two together.

"Maybe we could go for a walk. Show me the pond I saw when we drove up?" She moved her hand and wrapped an arm around my shoulder. I let her, though I felt like stepping away.

We walked out together and were on the porch before I realized Wynn had disappeared.

"So, how are things with Nan?" Momma asked. "You like it here?"

"Fine. I like it just fine," I said. This was one of her standard questions, and it rubbed me the wrong way every time. "In fact, I like it a lot."

"Well, have you heard the new song? It's been getting some radio time. It's a duet with Brent

Chisholm. I sing it with him during the shows." That's as far as Momma's concern for me went—a few questions and back to her. "Not just backup anymore, sweetheart. This could really be it for me—for us. Maybe a solo album and TV appearances. I'm talking no more moving from place to place, no more rentals, no more sewing your own clothes, Jubi."

It showed how much Momma knew about me that she assumed I minded making my clothes.

"Brent is really helping me. He grew up in his dad's bait shop in a little Texas town like this one. He knows what it's like to struggle, just like us."

I dragged my feet along the gravel of our driveway. Momma talked like this every once in a while, like we were sisters who'd grown up together. Like the only thing separating us was an age difference and not a decision she made. Every year, there was always some opportunity that would lead to us being together more. And it never happened. A long string of almosts that led right to what kind of momma she really was versus the kind I wished she was.

"This moving all the time, it's not good for a kid," she said.

"But it's good for you?" I asked.

"Touring's different," she mumbled. "She moved your daddy a lot too." I shot her a look. She better not say a word against Nan or it'd be the last words she said to me tonight. Momma held her hands up. "I get it. Believe me, I do. After your granddad up and left and then your daddy..." She got quiet. The sounds of a country evening settled on us while the sun dipped below the horizon and lit the clouds orange.

She cleared her throat. "The song's called 'You Had It Wrong All Along.' Brent sings most of it. But I get to belt it out all on my own for almost a full minute if you add it all up. You sure you haven't heard it?" she asked.

I had, but I still shook my head.

Momma looked toward the pond and wrinkled her nose. "If it's all the same to you, this is as close to that pond as I'd like to get. Looks like the set of *Creature from the Black Lagoon*." She laughed but stopped when I didn't join in. The whole walk back, she talked on and on about recording booths and Brent Chisholm.

When we got to the house, Wynn was making scrambled eggs for dinner, and Nan sat at the kitchen table drinking a glass of juice. Wynn turned and said, "There are casseroles in the freezer, not much else. But no worries, Nan. I'll head to the grocery store first thing."

I glared at him. I knew for a fact we had marshmallows and instant oatmeal. Plus, I didn't want Momma getting the wrong idea. Nan and I were fine. We only needed a little help, not a full-force intervention. Besides, if Wynn had made Momma call me back like he said he would, she and Nan wouldn't be in such a twist.

"Well, I guess one of you can stay in Jubilee's craft room. And that couch folds out," Nan said. Wynn looked at Momma. It hadn't dawned on me that they'd stay with us. I certainly didn't want to give up my craft room when I'd hardly had a chance to call it mine.

"Nan, I won't be staying. Don't get me wrong, I want to," Momma said, reaching toward me. I pulled my hands off the table before she could grab hold of them. "But we've got Dallas in two nights, then Austin, Houston, Oklahoma City, and Tulsa. Wynn is going to stay with you, and trust me, there's no better person for it. As soon as this tour wraps up, I can be…more involved. But until then, you'll have my right-hand man." She motioned to Wynn, but he didn't smile at all, only stared out the front window.

Nan took a long drink of her juice and har-rumphed. I guessed she was suppressing a lot of quotes and probably a few almost-swears.

Whatever Momma meant by more involved, I'd drop dead of shock if anything changed. Momma didn't change, and she wasn't staying. I knew it, but suddenly I realized giving up my craft room wouldn't have killed me.

Before Wynn drove Momma back to Dallas, she leaned down and gave me a hug. Her hair fell over me, and for a half second, I remembered when I was a kid and we played peekaboo through the curling thicket of her hair.

"If you ever need anything, I'm only a phone

call away. I swear, you could ask me for anything at all, Jubi, and I'd be here," she insisted. She kissed my forehead, stepped up into the truck, and leaned out the open window. "I mean it."

I nodded, and they drove off. She'd said I could ask her for anything, but she never stayed long enough for me to know what I needed from her. I wasn't sure I really wanted her to stay, but I wasn't sure I wanted her to leave so soon either. It didn't matter, though, because she left and the words wouldn't come out anyway.

11

Donut Hole

Wynn was back by early morning making a show of flipping blueberry pancakes. Worse yet, he brought an air bed, meaning he didn't plan on taking the couch. While giving up my craft room for Momma might not have killed me, for Wynn, it just might.

I stood in the hallway surveying the kitchen scene when Nan said, "You know Alexandra. She talks big and makes promises to Jubilee, then never follows through. It's career first with her. It always has been. She left for good after

Clayton died, but she left plenty of times before that. I've made mistakes with Jubilee, but at least I've put her first."

When Wynn turned to face Nan, I backed into the bathroom doorway. "Things were different then. Lexie was grieving and fighting to get a foothold in a very tough industry. I won't pretend to know what's best for Jubilee. But I know you, Nan. I know you're always ready to move on to the next adventure, but to me, Jubilee seems ready to stay put."

Wynn tossed a pancake that landed with a hiss. I walked in and acted as if I hadn't heard a thing, and Wynn carried on like he was a regular in our kitchen.

"What do you two say to getting ready, going into town, and picking up some supplies to repaint these cabinets? If you want, I could talk to the landlord. I can't imagine anyone in their right mind would say no. Thought we'd also pick up some Greek yogurt too. It's packed with protein. Nan, you need your strength." Wynn flipped another pancake and then set a steaming stack of them on the table.

I didn't like the idea of Nan and Wynn having secret conversations behind my back, especially conversations that involved me. Just as I was working up the nerve to complain about things, including how I hated blueberries and had planned on working in my craft room until *someone* decided to camp out there, I saw Abby riding down our drive on her bike. She balanced a cardboard box across her handlebars with one hand.

"See you later, Nan!" I yelled over my shoulder and ran into the front yard like I'd been held prisoner.

Abby rode up and dropped the box on the ground. Inside were four cans of spray paint, painter's tape, and a staple gun.

"What's all this?" I asked.

"Well, something Arletta said stuck with me," she said. "'Crafters know crafting is fulfilling, but crafting alongside a good friend feeds the soul.' So, I thought we might fix up that bike together." She nodded in the direction of Wynn's pickup parked next to Nan's car. "Whose truck is that?"

"Just a family friend here to help out for a week or two." After her quoting Arletta, I felt like telling Abby the whole truth, but something stopped me. I never told other kids about my mother being a singer. Not since Alabama, where some kids found out and nicknamed me Donut Hole after Momma's song. That nickname stuck quicker than a coat of fast-drying decoupage.

Right then, Wynn came out carrying two glasses of lemonade and wearing a black shirt with blue embroidered flowers winding their way around his chest. Wynn's style was classic country chic.

"Thought you two might be thirsty." He waited and, after I neglected to make introductions, he asked, "This a friend of yours, Jubi?" Only Momma and Wynn called me Jubi, which was only slightly better than their retired Juju Beans of my earlier years.

"Abby, this is Wynn. Wynn, Abby," I said. "And it's Ju-bi-lee."

"All right, Ju-bi-lee," Wynn said, copying me, and I felt my eyes roll clear to my forehead. He smiled and handed me the two glasses.

"Thanks, and nice to meet you," Abby said.

He nodded and turned to leave. "Keep cool. It's going be another scorcher!" he hollered over his shoulder as he went back in the house.

"Family friend, huh? Two questions," Abby said. "Does he always dress like that and does he fish?"

I laughed. "Yes, and I haven't asked him." I tried to carry on as if family friends came dressed straight from the Grand Ole Opry stage every day. With my full attention on the box of supplies, I lifted a can of spray paint.

"Abby, these are great, but they're all shades of brown. Except this one called Avocado," I said. "So, a greenish brown." I was joking—sort of.

"Yep, those are the colors of the sign Dad made for the One Stop. He never throws anything away," she answered. She used the heel of her sneaker to kick at a mound of dried grass in our yard, our avocado-colored yard. "But if you want different colors, that's fine."

"Let's definitely fix it up together." I didn't want to hurt Abby's feelings. "We could use the brown. The brown is fine. And Avocado is great. Arletta would call it an earthy tone." She quit kicking dirt and smiled.

"Hardware store opened at nine. Want to go?" she asked. "It's your bike. You should get to pick whatever colors you want."

I figured there was only one hardware store—Hope Springs Hardware, where Holly's nephew Colton worked.

We got permission to ride into town, along with some spending money from Nan. As we were about to leave, Wynn motioned me over and held out more money. "You'll need more than one can. And be sure to get some primer, sandpaper to use on the frame before you spray it, and some kind of sealant or lacquer if you want it to really shine. If you guys could stand to wait a few minutes, Nan and I could go with? I need some supplies for the cabinets. Plus, I know a little about bikes."

I shook my head and took the folded-up bills. "Not enough room in your truck," I answered, ignoring the fact that we could take Nan's car.

"Thanks," I yelled as Abby and I ran out the door. Wynn could use those fancy boots to make a mad dash all the way back to Dallas. I suspected he was only here as Momma's spy. Besides, with him holed up in my craft room, I had no choice but to craft at the kitchen table like an amateur again.

Hope Springs Hardware was covered with signs advertising a "Sizzling Summer Sale" and free tickets to Griggs' Rigs Racing with any purchase. Abby swung the door open. Bells chimed and, from the back, someone yelled, "Colton! Customers!"

There he was, stacking box fans in a square of sunlight wearing faded jeans, a short-sleeved white T-shirt, and the same Texas Rangers cap.

"Hey, Colton. We need some spray paint," Abby said.

"And some sandpaper," I added.

"What grit?" he asked without looking away from his boxes.

"What what?"

Colton smiled. "Different sandpaper for different jobs," he explained.

"We're fixing up that old bike of mine," Abby said. He walked us over to a wall with stacked trays, all neatly organized, and pulled out two sheets of rough paper, handing them over to me. He pointed to a locked cabinet on the back wall full of spray paint. "Need the key."

He walked off, and Abby grabbed my arm. "That's weird," she whispered. "I've been friends with Colton Griggs my whole life, and I have *never* heard him talk that much. But we mostly go fishing, and I don't like a lot of chitchat."

Colton returned with the keys. "Need primer?" He handed me a can and looked straight at me. "You'll need this too, if you want it to shine." His eyes were brown, not dirt brown, but bronze—

penny brown. I nodded. He handed me two cans of spray lacquer.

"Takes a week to set, but it'll look like a mirror." Then, I swear, he winked. Or maybe it was a blink, and I was just focused on one eye.

We picked out three colors: aqua, pale yellow, and a bright green. As Abby stowed our supplies in her backpack, I noticed Holly's car in front of the Fabric Barn. It'd be nice to stop by and say hi. Plus, I knew the perfect oilcloth print for the bike seat. Abby and I started off walking and ended up racing down the sidewalk before busting into the store in a fit of giggles.

Rayburn didn't bark at the commotion, and Holly wasn't in her normal spot. She paced in front of the phone. I hustled to aisle three, slipped out the roll of green oilcloth printed with lemon slices, and walked up to the cutting counter. Holly hadn't noticed us at all, so I cleared my throat.

"Oh, Jubilee. You working today?" she asked.

"No. Just need half a yard of this," I said.

"Well, go ahead. I'll start you a tab." After

I made the cut, I folded the fabric, and Holly waved us out without another word.

"Wonder what's with her today?"

"Rayburn's at the vet. They're not sure what's wrong with him this time. Could be anything. Last year, he ate a whole box of buttons, Holly's house key, and a block of cheddar cheese. You never smelled anything so awful," Abby said. "When your mom's the mayor, you hear everything."

I was thinking about Holly and Rayburn, and wondering if there was some kind of craft that would make a gassy, hungry dog feel better, when I was hit by an idea so big that my ears almost shot off.

"Abby, that's it! Your mom's the mayor," I said.

"Yeah, I know." She narrowed her eyes.

"Maybe she could get us tickets to the Arletta Paisley show," I said. "Wouldn't that be great? To be right there in the audience."

"I don't know," Abby said. "Mom's not too high on Arletta and the SmartMart opening." That was all she said. She was quiet the whole bike ride back, not even glancing my way the entire trip. The closer we got to the rental house, the surer I was I'd done something wrong. I'd broken a top rule. Relocation Rule Number 7: Don't take or ask for anything big. But it wasn't breaking the rule that I was worried about. When I'd asked about the tickets, disappointment had flickered across Abby's face.

We hopped off our bikes and walked them up the drive. "It's too bad about Rayburn. I know some easy dog treats I could whip up and drop off tomorrow," I said. She smiled at me. I'd been so long without a true friend, or any friend, I'd forgotten how to act like one. Maybe taking didn't have anything to do with it at all. Maybe the problem was Nan and I never gave much of anything back. The Relocation Rules we'd come up with only seemed to work if we thought about no one but ourselves.

"Rayburn was a present from Holly's husband. He passed a few years ago," she said. "Holly used to win quilting contests and have classes that drew quilters from all over the state.

But after Mr. Paine died, she quit doing all that." Abby and I hopped off our bikes and walked them through the front yard.

I dropped my bike as soon as I saw Wynn. He came out with a collapsed cardboard box and a lawn chair. The shocking part was what he was wearing—athletic shorts, flip-flops, and a faded Brent Chisholm concert T-shirt. His legs were as pale as a plucked chicken.

"What?" he asked, unfolding the lawn chair and taking a seat. "Spray paint requires adult supervision. Put this box down so you don't paint the lawn." He tossed the box at me and looked around at our sorry yard. "On second thought, it might look better with a little bit of color. You know, Jubilee, we should seed this yard. Soil's blowing away because there's nothing holding it down."

Abby and I dumped our supplies on the ground.

"Hmm. Probably should start with a base coat," I said, ignoring Wynn.

"Hang on." He hopped up from the chair. "Let me take some stuff off. If you're working with

146

just the frame, it'll be easier." He headed to the shed and came back with a rusty toolbox. The bike lay disassembled in less than ten minutes.

"How'd you do that?" I asked.

"My uncle owned a repair shop. I can fix about anything, from toasters to cars. But when I was a kid, I ran my own side business fixing up bikes. Now, you're right about a base coat. That's what the primer is for."

"I know that," I said and snatched the can of primer.

"First, you need to sand it," Wynn added.

I glared. Wynn backed away with his hands up, and I bit down a smile.

After we sanded, sprayed on the white primer coat, and let it dry, the morning had passed without us noticing. Wynn made peanut butter sandwiches dripping with jelly. Then, with sticky fingers washed, Abby and I started out with the lighter aqua color, and before long Wynn was hunched over the frame, helping. We laughed and talked, and Wynn ran back and forth for refreshments in between Nan hollering suggestions and inspiring quotes from the porch. Wynn had a laugh that sounded like a horse neigh, and it made us giggle even harder.

Finally, Nan called it quits. "That's it. You all need a break and I need some company." Wynn grabbed a kitchen chair from inside for her to sit in, helping her hobble down the steps, then ran back into the kitchen and brought out two shallow baking dishes and a box of sodas. Nan looked at the deconstructed bike and then back and forth between Abby and me. "Jubilee, I think this is some of your best work. Louisa May Alcott said, 'It takes two flints to make a fire.' It's going to be a beautiful bike."

"Might have taken three flints in this case." Abby nodded toward Wynn, who was crouched over the baking pan.

He poured a few Cokes into the pan, then soaked the chain and the handlebars. Abby and I stared with our mouths open. "Phosphoric acid in Coke removes rust," he explained. He raised the piece that held the chain and looked like a big gear. "This is your crankset. We can soak it too. It'll look like new, and if it doesn't, we can order you a replacement."

"Well, I never knew Coke was good for anything but drinking," Nan said, and Wynn handed out all the extra sodas, not leaving one for himself.

"I'll let these soak for a while. We got time, anyways. Takes about a week for the lacquer to set. When it does, we can put it all back together."

"Thanks, Wynn," I said.

"One last thing," he said, and then took off at a trot toward the shed. He came back with a small wicker basket. "Saw this when I was looking for tools. What do you think about putting it at the base of the handlebars?"

"It's going to be perfect," I said. Then I gave Abby the biggest hug I'd ever given anything that wasn't a stuffed animal.

"You're welcome. Easy on my casting arm," she teased.

I let go, and we both laughed.

I turned to Wynn. "It wouldn't have turned out so well if you hadn't helped."

"Well, it feels good to make something with the people I care about." He gave me a crooked smile. We all stood back and admired our work as the sun set behind us. Wynn put his arm around Nan for extra support, and she let him. I didn't think Arletta Paisley herself could have glamorganized that bike any better.

The frame was a clear ocean aqua, with the crank arms for the pedals and the handlebars painted pale yellow. Wynn had the idea to paint only the kickstand and the seat post bright green. It killed me a little that those bits of green were my favorite parts, what Arletta Paisley would have called the "perfect pop." And the lacquer made every piece glimmer like still water on a sunny day.

Nan was right; it was going to be a beautiful bike. And Wynn was right too. There was something different about sharing the feeling of making something, a feeling I normally kept for myself.

12

Never to Suffer

Since the lacquer would take a full week to dry, each day stretched longer than forever. Days and days with no bike meant relying on Wynn for rides—an inconvenience I hadn't considered and, according to Wynn, exactly what he was there for.

He liked to listen to the radio, loud and with the windows down. But he didn't just listen. He knew every country song ever created by heart and belted them all in a shrill wail the whole way to wherever we went. The singing only stopped when he paused to spit out the window, and he didn't care a bit how red I turned. Even though he was like a long-distance uncle to me, I'd never spent this much time with him. And sometimes, particularly when in his truck, I missed the distance.

When Wynn dropped me off at the Fabric Barn, I could still hear his howling. If Rayburn had been there, he might have joined in.

After two days, Rayburn finally came home from the vet. Wynn and I baked him a jar full of healthy dog treats. When I gave them to Holly, her eyes filled, she took my hand, and said, "Hiring you might have been the single smartest thing I've done in a long while." And then she kissed me on both cheeks.

For a minute, those kisses of Holly's shocked me stiff. I could count on one hand the people I allowed close to me. The longer we stayed in Hope Springs, the closer I got to needing another hand. And as much as I wanted to find our perfect place, I still wasn't positive this was it. Nan sure wasn't convinced. Getting too familiar meant getting hurt when we left. And we always left.

Arletta always said, "More often than not, the gift doesn't matter as much as the act of giving." I'd never stuck around long enough to see what Arletta meant until I gave Abby that paper fish. Which might mean I'd have to revise my firmly followed Relocation Rule Number 12: Give good gifts rather than goodbyes. It seemed like a lot of the rules Nan and I'd been living by could use a closer look, and I found myself hoping long and hard that a goodbye wouldn't happen anytime soon.

As I worked moving bolts of fabric from the back, I uncovered a dozen old sewing machines hidden by a stack of boxes. I walked up front with an armload of cotton prints.

"What's with all the machines in the back?" I asked.

"I used to teach classes before this place got so cluttered. Attendance dipped lower as I got messier. Just never started it up again." She stroked Rayburn and whispered into his flappy ear. "But who knows? Now that I've got some help..." Holly gave him another treat and lost her train of thought while scratching his head.

The sewing machines gave me an idea. "Holly, would you mind if I use one of those? Wynn's been helping out so much, especially with the cooking, I thought I might make him an apron."

"Sure. Whatever you need." She didn't take her eyes off Rayburn.

Once, I saw Arletta Paisley make a chef's apron on a show geared toward summer picnics and grilling. I'd just opened up Arletta Paisley's website on Holly's clunky old computer when I heard, "Oh, no you don't." Holly reached around me to close the window. "Let's make it together. I'll teach you how to modify a pattern."

As much as I trusted her, I suspected the offer had more to do with her dislike of Arletta than helping me. "Arletta cares about Hope Springs, Holly. She changed her whole show to help small towns."

"Jubilee, I appreciate your loyalty to her, but I bet every town she's stopping in is about to have or already has a SmartMart. It's a way for her to get rich and SmartMart to get richer, without having to look bad doing it." She motioned to the aisles. "I know it's a mess, but here in this store, I help folks create using what they've learned from real people. I taught what I learned from my mother and grandmother, not from a TV show or the computer."

"Well, some people don't have that." My voice was louder than I'd intended. I cleared my throat. "I mean, some people don't have family members with any crafting skills. So they have to teach themselves."

Holly sighed. "You're right, sweet girl. Of course, you're right about that." She studied the aisles again. "Times have changed, and you've half convinced me there's room for both ways."

The first time I'd gone to SmartMart, I'd been shopping for supplies for my very first Arletta Paisley project—embroidered handkerchiefs. The quote from that episode floated back to me now— "Hard times make the good times special"—a quote she'd hand-stitched on one cloth. I liked the idea that a little pain made life more interesting; I especially liked that Arletta felt the same way.

I crossed my arms. "Haven't you ever shopped at a SmartMart?"

"Before I noticed how many businesses were closing, I did. I'll only go now if I can't get what I need here in Hope Springs. Funny how many times it turns out I didn't really need it after all."

Holly riffled through the shelf of patterns, leaving me alone to think. Maybe she was saying that a true crafter made do, and part of the joy of crafting was creating without step-by-step directions and a kit. I'd have asked her more but was thrown off when she held up a pattern for a bib apron with a ruffled hem. "Here, with a few alterations, this'll do. We'll put a big pocket on the chest, adjust the waist, and leave the ruffle off."

I raised my eyebrows doubtfully.

"Come on, I'll help," she said. "Besides, patterns are a little like life. We take what we've got and make it suit our needs. We run the show."

Holly could alter, cut a pattern, and sew like

she was doing nothing harder than threading a needle. I picked out a fabric that looked like a black-and-white Holstein cow and a red bandanna print for the pocket and straps. With Holly's help, I finished the apron in about an hour.

I could hardly wait to give Wynn his gift. I wrapped it up in green tissue paper, tied a bright blue grosgrain ribbon in a bow around it, and slid it into a Fabric Barn bag. Had I ever given Wynn some sort of appreciation over the years? Not even a scrap. An apron was the least I could do.

After work, Wynn howled along with Carrie Underwood, and I sat in his truck with the baggie on my lap, unable to work up the nerve to give it to him. When we walked in, Nan was at our small kitchen table with Miss Esther, deep in conversation.

"After that, I did what I had to do to get by. Raised all three kids without a dime from their father," Miss Esther said.

Nan nodded. "Some heartaches never quite heal, do they?" she said quietly. This was not a quote or a Relocation Rule or anything else I'd ever heard her say before. Then she did something even more surprising. She patted Miss Esther's hand.

"Well, I better get going." Miss Esther stood. "See you this evening? I'll send my friend over around five and pick you up at seven."

"See you then," Nan said.

Miss Esther nodded to Wynn, and I swear, she winked at him. Then she said, "Good to see you again, missy." But I suspected she didn't mean that one bit.

She left on foot, moving at a sloth's pace toward the pond.

"What's going on? And did she walk here?" I asked. "Is that safe?"

"She stopped by to drop off more stuff and corner me into going out with her tonight. According to her, she walks a mile three days a week. And despite my saying no three times, she's sending her hairdresser over here."

"She's something else," I said.

"Oh, she's all right. Turns out we have a lot in common. How's Holly Paine doing?" Nan asked.

"Good. She sure knows how to sew. Can I help with anything?" I turned to Wynn, who was already in the kitchen setting up to fry pork chops.

"Nope, just want to make sure Nan eats something before her big evening out," he said.

"Someone's coming to fix your hair before dinner?" I asked, returning to our conversation.

"Yes, but I think I'll be able to do it myself soon. Today, I was able to get all the way dressed. And this thing"—she lifted her Aircast—"I'm starting to get used to it. 'Never to suffer would have been never to have been blessed.' Edgar Allan Poe."

"I could decorate it for you. Glue some sequins or rhinestones along the edge." I was already picturing Nan's brace gussied up, though she wasn't one for sequins—maybe silver studs.

"Sure." She leaned over to tuck a curl behind my ear. "This is a switch, huh? You taking care of me."

159

I shrugged. "It's not so bad. Seems like you've even had time to make a friend." I nodded toward the road where Miss Esther was still in sight.

Nan waved her good hand. "Oh, we're just going to a ladies' night bingo game at the Veterans' Center. I think Miss Esther's real reason for the visit was to check out Wynn."

Wynn yelled from the kitchen, "I was in the shower, and she stayed forever! I came out wrinkled as a prune. If I hadn't had to pick you up, I'd still be in there. Speaking of, I think there are actual prunes in that casserole she dropped off."

Nan laughed. "After thinking about her walking all the way here carrying that heavy casserole dish, I felt obligated to go tonight," she said.

I stayed in my room during Nan's home-visit beauty appointment. But when I came out for dinner, Nan looked like herself again, unmussed and dressed to impress in black leggings and a long red shirt with lipstick to match.

Wynn talked nonstop during supper. He talked about the weather, a stray dog he'd seen, the pond, the size of a mosquito he'd swatted, and new boots he wanted but couldn't afford. Since he'd moved in, he'd been to the grocery store, cleaned, cooked every meal, and even planted some sunflowers in front of the house.

"I got the go-ahead from Dr. Burgess. I'm going to start on this kitchen tomorrow," he added. "I'll have to take all the hardware off, sand down the cabinets, and prime everything before we can even think about a first coat of paint. I could use some help. What do you say, Jubi—I mean, Jubilee?"

I nodded without making any outright commitments. Nan shot me a look.

While Wynn put away the dishes, singing again, Nan leaned over with effort and whispered, "He doesn't have to be here, you know. And he really is a help."

Wynn's voice floated out to us. "You know, Nan, I was talking to Jubilee about buying some grass seed for the yard. You're losing your topsoil because there's nothing rooted down." He stopped crashing dishes to look at us. "It's good to have roots. Gives the soil something to hold on to, and it's nice to watch something you've planted grow."

We both knew he wasn't only talking about our yard—he was talking about our relocation habits too.

Nan straightened herself in the chair and avoided my told-you-so look when a knock sounded at the front door. I opened it to Miss Esther coated in as much hairspray, jewelry, and makeup as Miss Universe. She squinted her eyes and frowned at me, clearly disappointed in her greeter.

"Where's the friend of the family?" she whispered.

"Wynn! Miss Esther's asking for you!" I yelled then gave Miss Esther a big smile. "Come on in."

She squinted her eyes even smaller and shuffled in.

"Well, Nan Johnson, you look better than when I last saw you." She gave a nod of approval and scanned the house. "I meant to say earlier, before you shot out of here, that the new touches look nice. I suppose this is your doing?" she said to Wynn.

"I only keep an eye on things and cook. Jubilee does most of the heavy lifting and every bit of the decorating. Really, in a week or so, I don't think they'll need me at all," he said. Now that he'd brought it up, I realized while I didn't love the idea of him living in my craft room, I didn't love the idea of him leaving either.

"Wynn, you can't stay in the house all day. I'll be by tomorrow around noon and you can help me make my rounds," Miss Esther said. "We'll go by the First Baptist Church and help with the food drive, and then we can stop in on a quilting circle at the nursing home. Oh, they'll get a kick out of you." She motioned to Wynn, whose eyes widened with fear. "And I have some cuttings from my garden I can help you plant."

"I'll definitely take those cuttings," Wynn said. "We were just talking about getting something rooted and growing in the front yard." Nan shot him a look. "But we've made plans to repaint the kitchen. So I'll be busy here for the next few days."

"Yeah, too bad," I said and earned my own look from Nan.

"I can't figure why you'd want to paint the cabinets, but whatever butters your biscuit." Miss Esther pointed at Nan. "Let's get a move on before someone steals my regular seat. Fridays fill up faster than an Easter basket."

She honked twice before they pulled out of the driveway and sped away in a shower of gravel. Wynn and I watched from the window, and Nan looked at us wide-eyed as she struggled to buckle her seat belt.

"You think she'll be okay with that lady?" I asked.

"I sure hope so," he said. "She seems pretty alert for her age."

"Yeah, alert, like a stirred-up rattlesnake," I said.

"One with a lot to rattle," Wynn added, and we both laughed.

"Well, I better take care of the rest of those dishes." He turned to leave.

"I'll help, but wait a second. I made something for you." I ran to get the gift from my room. Wynn took it, sat down at the table, and held it for a bit, smiling down at the wrapping. He grabbed the ribbon, ready to pull, but then stopped and looked at me.

"I'll make you a deal. I'll open this if you open the last letter your momma sent."

I crossed my arms. "How do you know I don't read them?"

"I know because, if you read them, you might not be so angry, might even forgive her a little bit. I know she dragged you through a bad time, but she's not a bad person. And she loves you. I know you and Nan are quick to part with places, but people ought to be harder to let go of. Don't you think?"

All the warm feelings I'd been fostering all

afternoon shriveled up and froze solid. I pointed at the package. "It's an apron," I said. Then I stood and walked out of the room.

Nan once told me that my mom's heart had been broken by my daddy's death. So broken that she couldn't put it back together on her own, and that she'd moved into a place to get help. That was three years ago, the same time Momma's first letter arrived. Along with it came a package of papers from her attorney for Nan to sign, making Nan my official guardian.

Just like that, Momma had given me up. I wasn't the one who let go.

More than thirty envelopes in various shades of pink sat stacked in an old shoebox. Whatever those letters said, it wasn't enough.

RAYBURN'S HEALTHY DOG TREATS

Level: Intermediate

Supplies:

* 2 cups whole wheat flour

* 2 4-oz. jars organic baby food, pureed carrots or sweet potato (be sure the food contains no spices—some can cause an allergic reaction, or in Rayburn's case, unwanted gastrointestinal activities)

* Twine

* Gift tag

* Mason jar

Tools:

* Mixing bowl

* Wooden spoon

* Rolling pin

* Cookie cutters (keep the size on the small side, but any shape goes—from the classic bone, to hearts, to fire hydrants)

* Parchment paper

* Black marker

Directions:

1. **Preheat** oven to 350°F.

2. In a mixing bowl, use a wooden spoon to stir all the ingredients until they form a thick dough.*

3. On a lightly floured surface, roll out the dough to about ¼-inch thickness. Cut with cookie cutters and transfer to a cookie sheet lined with parchment paper.

4. Bake for 20 minutes.

5. When completely cool, place the treats in a jar, wrap twine around the lid, and label the gift tag.

* Wynn and I added a teaspoon of ginger for Rayburn's upset stomach.

13

Play It Safe

Saturday morning, Nan looked almost like her old self. Wynn made lumpless oatmeal, and I noticed the apron still wrapped and sitting on the kitchen counter. Nan reached over and plopped a handful of mini-marshmallows and a heaping spoon of brown sugar in my bowl when his back was turned, but I still didn't eat a bite.

"Jubilee, I know we just got here, but talk about starting off on the wrong foot." Nan held up her Aircast. "I think, after I mend and before I even start this new job, we might need to change course. We could lose our security deposit, but I'm not sure I care. Besides, your momma is really breathing down my neck this time. I called Mr. Taft and our apartment is still vacant. It's ours if we want it."

Move back? We hadn't even finished unpacking, and she was ready to call it quits. Wynn crashed pots around in the sink. I didn't say a word.

"Onward and upward. Or in this case, backward." She raised her glass of juice like she was giving a toast and gulped it down.

"But we just got here," I said. I'd had such high hopes for Hope Springs, and it was looking to be our shortest stay yet. "I can't believe this." I whispered that last part, barely said it out loud, but with it came all the past doubts and frustrations bubbling up on their way to my mouth.

"There's no use sugarcoating it. Your mom is serious this time. But we've got a few choices that might help smooth things over. Move right next to her, to some town just outside Dallas, or move back. You can start at the same school after summer, like we never left." Nan squeezed my hand gently. "Think about it. If we move back, she might give up trying to get you to live with her. Knowing your momma, she'll probably cool off or get distracted. We might not need to worry about it at all."

Get me to live with her? I didn't say another word for the rest of breakfast. Everything I was about to say was swept clean out of my head, blown away by the idea of Momma wanting me back.

I stayed silent in Wynn's truck all the way to town, a lump in my throat, refusing to say a word. Though, with him belting out every song, he hardly seemed to notice. When we pulled up to the Fabric Barn, he turned off the radio.

"Want to talk about it?" he asked. I wasn't sure which "it" he meant—Momma's letters and now her interference, him acting like a spoiled baby and not opening my gift, or Nan and our next move.

"Did you know about Momma causing trouble?" I asked.

"No. I knew she was worried," he said. "Lately, your mom and I haven't been seeing eye to eye. But believe it or not, I know Nan pretty well. She loves you more than anything, and she'll figure this out."

"*We'll* figure it out. Nan and me, I mean." I hopped out and slammed the door.

After he drove off, I headed down the block to the front of the Hope Springs post office and plopped down on a bench. The deserted stoplight creaked as it swung, and that little lonesome moan of a sound broke open whatever was already cracked inside me. I cried smack in the middle of town, and I didn't care who saw. Somewhere in my heart, under all the anger and disappointment, I'd wished for Momma to want me back. I'd wished for a perfect place too. Who knew that one wish coming true meant the other couldn't?

I wiped my face, took a deep breath, and walked down the block to the Fabric Barn.

Holly and I didn't talk much that morning. I sorted the new notions and tried to organize a button display. I'd sifted through seven boxes of different-sized tortoiseshell buttons when Abby came bursting through the door, huffing air like she'd run a marathon.

"I rode as fast as I could," she said. "Mom just told me this morning."

"Told you what?" I asked.

"She got three tickets to Arletta's show in Hope Springs. And she says we can have them. They're filming next Monday!"

I didn't let her say another word before I screamed, then she screamed, and Rayburn started howling. Abby and I laughed, and even Holly smiled a little. It didn't last long, though.

"Abby, I'm surprised at you," she said. "I'll bet you my whole store it's a matter of time before everyone starts buying cheap fiddle-faddle from SmartMart rather than paying a little more for something from their own neighbors."

"Holly, I'll take your bet," I said. "She's the southern Martha Stewart, not Darth Vader, and somehow I'm going to prove it to you." I wasn't sure of much, but dang it, I still believed in Arletta Paisley. Maybe she wasn't perfect, but no one was. "I won't take the whole store. Maybe a bolt of any fabric I want against me cleaning the rest of that backroom free of charge?"

"If Arletta's not up to something, you can have free fabric for life," Holly said.

"Deal," I agreed, then grabbed Abby's hands and swung her around until Rayburn barked and skittered across the floor trying to join us.

Arletta Paisley and I had been through some tough times together. I knew her kitchen better than I knew my own family tree, and I thought I knew a little of her heart. I was convinced she cared—about Hope Springs and about making life better with effort and an eye for detail. I just had to convince Holly I was right.

"Well, keep Rayburn out of it," Holly said.

I shrugged, Abby laughed, and we danced around my newly glamorganized button display. Abby was dancing more for my sake than her own, and that felt almost as good as getting those tickets.

Holly shook her head at us. "If Arletta makes you two this happy, then maybe she's not all bad."

I ran over and hugged her, feeling like at least this battle was half won, even if the rest of my life was a mess.

The Rally

"The way I see it, we've got two choices." Abby paced while I lay on the soft green rug in her bedroom. The fish I'd made her hung from the chain on her ceiling fan. Her brothers sat beside me coloring, Harrison quietly and Garfield not so quietly.

"If I was a Transformer, my name would be Laser Boom. Harry's would be Silent Thunder, and Abby's would be Sassy Beans. What would yours be, Jubilee?" Garfield asked.

"I don't know. But I'll seriously think about

it," I said. Harrison nodded and studied me as though he was already considering options.

"We can ask my mom or Nan or my dad. Or Wynn, if you want. You know, keep the extra ticket in the family." Abby was good at planning. Instead of a headboard, a spreadsheet stretched behind her bed, pushpins tracking her best catches. She'd charted times, dates, and weather conditions (including degree of cloud cover) for each fishing trip to Lake Trenton, the site of her next competition.

I'd spent the night planning too. Before I fell asleep, I lay there hunting for a way to prevent another move so soon.

Searching for the perfect place had always felt like an adventure, kind of like a fairy-tale quest. It wasn't until two moves ago—when we left Blessed, Alabama—that I regretted leaving. Last night, just thinking of it again had given me an idea—a big idea. Still, an hour into being at Abby's, I hadn't found the right time to tell her.

"Or we could branch out. Maybe ask, I don't know...Colton?" she asked. My stomach fluttered.

"I like Colton," Garfield said. "He has a race-track." At that, the twins jumped up and ran from the room roaring like race cars.

I sat up. "Would he even want to go?"

"My guess is he'll go if you go," she said, and waggled her eyebrows up and down.

I ignored her and jumped at the opportunity to change the subject. "I've been thinking. All my old schools had pep rallies for the football team, no matter how badly they played. Could we do something like that for the town?"

Now was as good a time as any to tell her my plan; maybe it'd get my mind off Colton and the odd feeling I got every time someone would say his name, I'd ride by the hardware store, use my fancy glue gun, or think of baseball, box fans, or blue jeans. I still needed to prove to Holly that Arletta Paisley and SmartMart weren't out to ruin the town. Plus, I knew what mattered to Abby. She loved Hope Springs, and if I was going to leave, at least I could show her I cared too.

"You saying Hope Springs stinks?" Abby asked.

"No. No, I'm saying—I just meant that..."

She started laughing before I could explain myself.

"You really want to do something for the town?"

"Sure," I said. "We could remind everyone to support small businesses. As long as customers keep shopping in town, then Hope Springs has a chance to compete against SmartMart."

"It's just, well, it seems like you guys move a lot. Why would you want to help?" She looked straight at me, right into my eyes. And I decided to tell her a little of the whole truth.

"I hope we don't move anytime soon. Everyone's been so nice. I'd like to give something back." As I said it, I hoped with every inch of me that this wouldn't be a parting gift.

She jumped up. "You just gave me an idea. Like my dad says, strike while the griddle's hot." She clapped her hands the way a gym teacher would. "Let's go."

Taking her lead, we parked our bikes in front of Hope Springs Hardware.

I was so nervous, I straightened my skirt four times before Abby said, "Don't worry. He likes you too." Then she walked in and left me frozen on the sidewalk for several seconds before following her.

Colton was arranging a pyramid of power drills right beside the front door. On the display was another sign for 20 percent off. Sale signs were stationed all over the store and taped on the windows too. Colton nodded at us when we walked in.

"What's with all the sales?" Abby asked.

"SmartMart coming. Dad wants to build up customer loyalty," he said, and continued stacking boxes.

"Speaking of SmartMart. We have a plan to save Hope Springs," I said.

"You want in?" Abby asked.

He lowered the box he held and gave us his full attention.

"Jubilee had an idea back at the house. Tell him." Abby nodded at me.

"You know how the high school always has

pep rallies for teams with a big game coming up? Helps everybody feel good. Gives them hope, especially when they're facing someone with a way better record?"

Colton nodded.

"Well, what if we did something like that for the town?" I asked.

"Almost every kid I know spends part of Saturday at Griggs' Rigs Racing," Abby said.

"What if we got businesses to have booths, got some restaurants to set up a few stands and sell food, and maybe some giveaways or a contest?" I added.

"Cheer everyone up and remind them to shop local. You think your dad would go for it?" Abby asked.

Colton nodded again.

"It'll take some signs, community outreach, organizing, and planning. But I think we could do it. And maybe my mom could help." Abby switched to a whisper. "I'm even thinking of bottling up free samples of my dip bait."

"My brothers and I can handle the booths.

Take just the cost of the lumber," he said. That was a yes! I bit my lip to keep a squeal from escaping. "But charge for the dip bait," Colton added.

Abby whooped, high-fived Colton, and then gave me a hug. We planned to meet the next evening at the One Stop and work out the details, given Colton's dad agreed. I was so excited and full of jitters the rest of the afternoon that Nan suggested we lay off the marshmallows.

The next morning, I arrived at the Fabric Barn a little late because Wynn insisted I eat breakfast. With as few words as possible, I asked him to drive me to the One Stop later in the evening and he agreed. Things were stiff between us, and the apron still sat all wrapped up on the kitchen counter.

He dropped me off, and before I reached the door of the Fabric Barn, I could hear Holly yelling. I rushed forward and was almost knocked over by a man fleeing. Holly burst out after him, holding a broom over her head and yelling, "Don't you dare come back! I'm calling every business in town to let them know what you look like. Some carry more than brooms, mister!"

The man ran across the street, jumped into a burgundy sedan, and peeled out down Main Street.

"Thief or old friend?" I asked.

"Ha! I think he was a SmartMart scout," she said and began sweeping the sidewalk in front of the store. "Had a notebook, taking notes on your 'best sellers' display. My brother called yesterday and said something similar happened at the hardware store and gave me a description of the same guy. Also said you kids were scheming something fierce in the front of the store." Sounded like Mr. Griggs talked a lot more than his son and had a bad case of paranoia in common with his sister.

I shrugged, not ready to let her in on the plan yet.

"Now I have to call every local business and tell them about this scout. Stop him before he does his dirty work." She smacked the broom three times before going inside.

I followed. "I'll do it, Holly."

She stopped and eyed me suspiciously. "All right. I have a good old-fashioned phone book under the counter."

I scribbled down a script to fight off my nerves. The first call on the list was the one I was most worried about.

My fingers shook as I dialed.

"Hope Springs Hardware," a voice I knew was Colton's answered.

"Hi, Colton. It's Jubilee. Did your dad say yes?" I asked.

"Yep," he said.

"Okay. Well, I'll start calling other businesses."

"Okay," he said.

"See you later." I waited.

"Yep," he said again and then hung up. If he liked me, he sure wasn't showing it with words.

I pushed buttons and all thoughts of Colton out of my head—at least I tried to—and dialed every auto supply, hair salon, pharmacy, antique store, grocery, and diner in town. Every business, whether I thought they'd be affected or not, got a call. I asked if they'd be interested in participating in the first-ever Celebrate Hope Springs Rally at Griggs' Rigs Racing.

When Holly noticed I wasn't bringing up any theories about SmartMart scouts, she came over with a slight scowl, but as she listened in, her smile grew with each call I made. I kept a list of businesses that said yes, promising to get back to them soon with more details.

When I hung up, Holly stood right beside me looking ready for a hug. Instead, I asked, "Holly Paine, as a local business owner, would you be interested in participating in the first Celebrate Hope Springs Rally?"

She shook her head, her smile spreading even wider. "You are full of surprises. A rally is just the boost this town needs. But I'm still calling to warn people about that scout." She picked up the phone again, but then paused and said, "I thought you were a dedicated Arletta Paisley and SmartMart supporter. What's changed your mind?"

I thought about her question for a minute.

I couldn't say it was only because of Abby, or because Colton agreed to help, or that planning and working on something with the two of them felt about a hundred million times better than doing it alone. So I said, "I don't think it's going to make that much difference to SmartMart one way or the other. But I do think it's important for the people of Hope Springs to be reminded of what they already have, instead of what new thing might be further down the road. And if Arletta believes what she says on her shows, I think she'd be proud of what Abby and Colton and I are doing. Plus, I've got a lifetime of free fabric on the line." I winked to let her know I was only half joking.

Holly laughed. "Well, you're right about that, I guess."

Before I left that day, Holly loaded me up with vintage fabric she had left from her opening year. I knew those bolts were special to her, and she knew they'd be special to me. She walked me to the door. "Now that the back looks so much better, I've decided to start teaching classes again. First one is in three days. I'd be less nervous with you there, but I understand if you're busy."

"I wouldn't miss it." She hugged me again and waved from the door as I piled into Wynn's truck with all my loot.

The front seat was so filled with fabric and country music and Wynn's singing that I wondered if he'd noticed I hadn't said a word during our rides for the past few days.

"So, what are you up to lately?" he asked.

I stared out the window. "Same old, same old."

"Doesn't seem like same old to me," he said. "Seems a little different."

I bit my lip and stayed quiet the rest of the ride. As soon as the truck rolled to a stop, I jumped out and ran for the house. Nan stood by the front windows like she'd been waiting for us.

I swung open the front door, and there was my new bike, all set up in the living room like a little kid's Christmas present. Wynn had attached the basket, and a matching aqua ribbon wove its way through the basket's top lattice and ended in a bow right in the front. Even in pieces I'd known the bike was going to look amazing, but it looked better than I'd imagined, better than perfect.

"You like it?" Nan asked. "Wynn put it together. I'm only responsible for the ribbon."

"I love it," I said. I gave her a gentle hug, and before I knew it, I was giving Wynn a squeeze too.

15

Top-to-Bottom Right

When I took my bike on its first spin, my hair blew in my face as wild primroses and bluebells flashed pink and purple along the fence. Texas Red Oaks lined our road and dappled the hills, and the summer trill of bugs and sweet grass filled the air. That gussied-up bike was a new kind of freedom.

Wynn was right. It was different here. *I* was different here.

The gravel crackled under my wheels as I braked in our driveway. With one foot on the ground and the other resting on my bike, I took a minute to stare at our raggedy little rental and felt so full of hope that I wanted to stand there and feel like that forever. But there was a meeting to prepare for. I stopped short as soon as I stepped foot inside.

Wynn and Nan waited in the living room. Nan wore makeup, her skinniest, blackest jeans, and her biggest hoop earrings. She must have let Wynn fix her hair, because the style looked a little too similar to his own. Wynn wore dark jeans and a white Western shirt with bright yellow panels surrounded by brown piping, paired with matching brown leather boots. Hair gel, perfume, aftershave, and a hint of shoe polish almost knocked me over.

"Wow," I said, looking between the two of them. I knew Nan and Wynn shared a past, but it looked like they shared a sense of fashion too. "Wow." It was a double wow kind of situation.

Nan smiled. "Wynn says he'd like to take us out for dinner to Frank Standridge's place downtown. Won't it be nice to go out for a change?"

Wynn gave me a one-sided smile. That wasn't the deal we made on the way home, and he knew it. I was supposed to come home, wash up, eat with them, and then he'd agree to drive me—and only me—to meet with Abby and Colton. It was a business meeting, not a dinner date. He was up to something.

"I thought it'd be fun for the whole family to go," he said. That word—family—almost took my breath away. Was that what we were? Me and Nan and Wynn.

Nan said, "Why don't you go freshen up? And then we'll head out." She looked better than she had since her fall, and maybe happier than I'd seen her in a long while. I'd no option but to go to my room to get ready.

On the drive to town, Wynn looked over at Nan and said, "You remember that time Clay and I rode our bikes straight through old man Hodges's yard and into his pool?"

She laughed. "I do. As I recall, it was in the middle of his daughter's birthday party?"

"Well, a stunt like that requires an audience,"

Wynn said. He glanced at me in the rearview mirror. "Clay was a lot like you, Jubilee—full of ideas. But he didn't talk about them much. I think he liked to open his heart more than his mouth."

Clay was my dad's name. Clayton, really. Nan rarely talked about him, and only if I asked. I didn't ask often, because I thought remembering made her heart ache. Something about this particular memory made her shake her head, stifle a laugh, and stare out the window with a wide smile—like the opposite of an ache, more like a relief.

I looked up front at Wynn, driving and smiling in that same kind of comforted way. I'd always thought of him as getting in the middle of things, squeezing between me and everyone I cared about. But maybe he was more like glue trying to hold everyone together.

The One Stop was packed, with only three barstools open at the counter. Wynn decided Nan wouldn't be comfortable without back support, a claim she denied, but then agreed to wait for a booth all the same. We stood by the cash register until Abby's dad exited the kitchen wearing a stained apron and a backward baseball cap.

"You must be the famous Nan." He wiped a hand on his apron before offering it to her. "And you must be the equally famous Wynn."

"We've really enjoyed getting to know Abby," Wynn said, giving him a hearty handshake. "She's a good friend to our Jubilee."

OUR Jubilee! The more those two words rang in my head, the more I thought about family. It didn't have to be only me and Nan. Wynn rested his palm on my back. When I met his eye, he gave me a wide smile.

Abby's dad took Nan by the arm and led her to a booth. A booth! Nan and I were always seated at tables, booths being reserved for parties bigger than two. All of a sudden, it seemed like the air conditioner had quit working. Happiness heated me up until my fingertips tingled. I glanced over at Nan to see if she felt the same. Her smile told me she did.

"I know you've had a rough introduction, so let's make this your official welcome to Hope Springs. I say you start with dessert and work your way backward. I have a marshmallow chocolate cream pie that's to die for," Abby's dad said. Nan nodded, and I could tell she was impressed. Though I didn't want her to be reminded of going backward, I wondered if Abby'd mentioned Nan's marshmallow affinity or if the whole Standridge family was simply double-dosed with some sort of sixth sense when it came to hospitality.

Wynn offered Nan a seat, and I hoped all this princess treatment was softening her opinion of Hope Springs. Despite Abby's dad's suggestion, we each picked a main course to start. Nan and I chose the chicken-fried steak, and Wynn ordered bacon-wrapped meatloaf. The food was so good, we barely said a word to each other while we ate.

When Wynn finished, he rubbed his stomach and said, "I like it here. Not just the restaurant, but the whole town. You know what it reminds

me of? A smaller version of Tullahoma, Tennessee. Don't you think, Nan?"

She finished her last bite and slid the plate
forward. "My word, I think I haven't left any
room for that pie. Frank was right; I should
have worked backward." She skillfully ignored
Wynn's question. Tullahoma was where Momma
and Wynn had grown up, where my daddy had
gone to high school, and where I was born.

Wynn went on, unfazed. "I bet we can find
some room," he said and motioned to our waiter.
"Three slices of the marshmallow chocolate
cream pie, please."

"So, Jubilee, what's this I hear about you
organizing some kind of rally?" Nan asked.
"Miss Esther stopped by this afternoon and said
you'd called everybody in town. Frankly, I think
she's miffed she wasn't included. Believe me, the
woman knows every soul, living and passed on,
in the whole county." From the look on Nan's
face, Miss Esther wasn't the only one miffed at
being left out.

"I was going to tell you, Nan," I said. "Everybody in town is worked up about the SmartMart opening. Holly's dead-determined that Arletta Paisley's out to close her business. So, Abby and I thought it would be nice to have sort of a get-together to remind everyone to support local stores. You know, make them feel better," I said. "We need all the help we can get."

Nan softened a bit. "If you need my help, sweetheart, I'm here to give it." Nan always went along with my projects, but this rally was worlds different than putting up removable wallpaper or braiding our own rag rugs.

The waiter arrived with three slices of pie and said, "Dessert is on the house."

"See?" Wynn said. "Can't beat a place that gives out free pie."

"But it's not like you to get so wrapped up in local concerns," Nan said, fixing me with her eyes. This was exactly why I hadn't told her about the rally in the first place.

"I think it's great to get involved. Being part of a community is what makes a place a home,"

Wynn chirped and then avoided Nan's glare. Nan and I never called any place we lived our home; it was always "this town" or "this place"— sometimes something worse.

Nan shifted uncomfortably in her seat. It was hard to tell if it was her ribs bothering her or the conversation.

"I'm just worried, that's all." She gave me a long look, and I could tell exactly what she was thinking. She'd taught me to always think of a way out, an escape route, and getting this deep into something made getting back out a whole lot trickier.

Just then, Garfield burst through the door and yelled, "Daddy! I need a milkshake and some bacon, STAT." Harrison followed closely behind, holding Abby's hand, and their mother herded the group forward.

Abby motioned me over to an empty booth by the kitchen.

"Go on," Nan said. "I'm a little worn out."

"I'll come get you in about an hour," Wynn said as he helped Nan out of the booth.

Nan waved to Abby's mom and said, "Tell Frank that's the best dinner I've had in years." If only each bite had pushed the maps further and further out of her mind.

Nan touched my arm, and that worried look washed over her face again. "I'm gonna call it a night. So, I'll see you in the morning. Maybe we could spend a little time together?" I nodded.

"See you soon," Wynn said. Then he leaned in and whispered, "Hard to think things won't work out after a meal like that." He waved as they left, and I watched him help Nan into our car.

As soon as I sat down, Abby slid across from me and mumbled, "Mom found out SmartMart got some incentive plan from the governor. They got the land at a reduced cost and don't have to pay the full property tax. I've never seen her so mad. She thinks they'll hire locals, work them just enough to avoid paying health insurance, and not give much of anything back to the town, aside from cheap goods and low-paying jobs."

"What's she going to do?" I asked.

"Not much she can do." Abby shrugged. "Just have to hope people don't shop there much. SmartMart can only do a lot of damage if we help them out."

I looked out the window and down Main Street with its line of parallel storefronts, one right up against the other. Through the glass, the setting sun painted all downtown in a golden glow. A familiar red double-cab truck rumbled up, and Colton hopped out wearing a grass-green John Deere T-shirt and a pair of faded jeans with a hole in the knee. Mr. Griggs stuck his head out the window and waved to him. I was in such a daze, I waved back.

I tried not to stare when Colton came in and walked toward us. But then he scooted into my side of the booth and caused me to lose all focus and concentration for several seconds. He nodded his hellos, and Abby shot me a not-too-subtle look, earning her a kick under the table.

"Ow!" she said and bent to rub her shin. Subtlety wasn't one of Abby's best qualities.

"So, what all did your dad say?" I asked.

"We can use the track. He'll even put on a race. All money from entry fees and tickets could go to the community Downtown Revitalization Fund," Colton said.

"There's a Downtown Revitalization Fund?" I asked.

Abby's mom appeared at our booth and scooted a chair over.

"There is now," she said. "Abby filled me in after Mr. Griggs called this afternoon and told me what you kids were planning, and I think it's brilliant. I'd like to help. I'm the mayor, after all."

We talked and talked and worked out a time-table for events. Colton confirmed he'd build the booths with his four brothers and his dad. Abby's dad said he'd set up a mobile One Stop food truck and would recruit other restaurant owners in town to do the same. I spent some time—a lot of time—distracted by the fact that Colton had four brothers. I kept imagining five of him, only different in size, like a good-looking set of nesting dolls.

"The town's really divided over this, and it's

only made worse now that SmartMart hired Arletta Paisley as their national spokesperson." I shifted in my seat as Abby's mom continued. "She's got a huge following." She rubbed her forehead. "But I'll call the paper and see what we can drum up in terms of coverage. We don't have a lot of time, but if we work smart and fast, we can pull off something special."

"We could have some craft tables for kids. And a raffle for a special wishing penny for the well. It'd be more gesture than anything else," I said. "That wishing well is the first thing I noticed when we came to town. Might be nice to remind people of it."

"Isn't Main Street Fest coming up? We already have a parade. What if the rally is right after? We'd get more people," Abby said. "Plus, the weekend before is the Family Pairs Bass Tournament. That always draws out-of-towners. If we advertise at the tournament, they might come back for the rally."

"And increase the sales of your stink bait!" I said.

"Dip bait," she and Colton said together.

Abby's mom leaned back and sighed. "Back when I was young like you three, Main Street Fest was really special, bigger than the Fourth of July. Events went on all weekend long. But with downtown businesses struggling to stay open, the festival got smaller and smaller until all we have left is the parade. I'd love to make Main Street Fest what it used to be."

"We can do it," Abby said. "Let's make Main Street Fest mean something again." Colton and I both smiled and nodded in agreement.

Abby's mom clasped both hands and said in a choked-up voice, "I don't think I've ever seen such a perfect moment of grassroots organization."

"Easy, Mom," Abby said.

We were still talking when Wynn's truck pulled in. I looked around and noticed the One Stop was empty other than our booth and Abby's family.

Main Street Fest was only a week and a half away, set to happen the weekend before Smart-Mart's grand opening. Colton decided how many booths to build based on the list I'd brought;

Abby's mom would handle local media coverage; and Abby's dad, along with lining up the food, knew a guy who'd make a banner for Main Street. I volunteered to make signs for all the businesses that wanted one. I also offered to make lollipops to sit by registers advertising the festival—free with purchase. Abby's mom said I had a real mind for business and suggested we call them rallypops.

"How'd it go?" Wynn asked once we were driving home.

"Really good," I answered. I was dying to get started on my posters and had already envisioned the perfect hand-lettered style. An old-fashioned circus font would be what Arletta called a "style-match made in heaven." I'd show Abby and Colton after I'd finished a few, and then we'd have copies made.

"Jubilee, I don't know if it means much, but I'm proud of you," Wynn said. He cleared his throat. "You're full of big ideas like your dad. And determined, like your momma."

He had on a classic country station and "Wide

Open Spaces" by The Chicks played as we drove. For once, Wynn didn't sing. "Got something from your mom today," he said.

Once, a record executive told Momma that her sound was too vintage, and "vintage meant over and done." Momma's voice was full, sweet and clear, but always cut through by a sad warble. I hated hearing her songs. That donut song almost ruined a whole year of my life. But it was more than that. Momma's voice called up the few memories I had of her—singing me to sleep, planting together with Nan in her old garden, the two of us driving in the car.

Momma sang when she was happy. She also sang when she was sad, and I had those memories too. In a way, I preferred the bad ones. It was easier to sort out how I felt about them.

As Wynn's Chevy lurched to a stop, he pushed a few buttons and a slide guitar intro began for what I could only guess was Brent Chisholm's duet with Momma. I started to open the door, but he gently grabbed my arm. "Just listen," he said. After a few verses of Brent singing, the chorus

started, and Momma's voice filled up every inch
of the truck.

> *If I counted up all my mistakes*
> *I'd have a list a mile high*
> *But my biggest regret by far*
> *Is leaving you behind*
>
> *You are my dusk, you are my dawn*
> *If that's not what you thought*
> *You've had it wrong all along*
>
> *I should have never left you at all*
> *Thought I was sparing us both some*
>   *pain*
> *Thought we'd be better off apart*
> *But I'm left with a you-shaped hole*
>   *in my heart*
>
> *You're in every thought, you're in*
>   *every song*
> *If that's not what you thought*
> *You've had it wrong all along*

"She wrote it, you know. She's written three of Brent's songs. But this one is her best." Wynn looked straight ahead. "Don't have to wonder too much about her inspiration."

"Why are you so loyal to her?" It was a question I'd wondered for years, but never had the nerve or the opportunity to ask. I could tell from the way his face crumpled that maybe I should've held off even longer.

"You know I grew up with your mom?"

I nodded.

"I lost my dad when I was sixteen, and my mom was a mess. Until I was old enough to move out, I lived with my best friend and his mom off and on—your dad and Nan. Your dad and mom fell in love, then you came along, and now here I am again. It felt like we were all in it together. The music was part of it, but more than that, it felt like family. Being a third wheel just comes natural to me, I guess." He cleared his throat. "I'm loyal because I respect her. I respect how hard she's worked to overcome what life's slung at her. I guess, it's that your momma did something mine couldn't. She struggled through her loss, and she did what was best for you, though it tore her up. I love her for doing that for you."

A song about partying with friends by Toby Keith came on the radio, and there couldn't have been a song that mismatched the mood more.

"Seems to me most people could use a third wheel," I said and was surprised by the catch in my voice. I'd known some of what Wynn had said, but not all of it. "I'll read one letter. But not tonight. Okay?" Then I was surprised again when he leaned over and smoothed down one of my flyaway curls before getting out of the truck.

"I wouldn't love you so much if you were a pushover," he called over his shoulder.

A rerun of Arletta Paisley's show was on that evening. Monday, Abby had shown up right before the live broadcast and almost dragged me out the door. She'd said there's no bad time to fish, but the best time to catch a catfish was at sunset. Sitting on that rotten dock, with the sinking sun lighting up the pond, was the first time I'd ever missed a new episode and now I was going to be late for the rerun.

I dashed to my room for my notebook, plopped onto the couch, clicked on the TV, and was greeted by a close-up of Arletta Paisley's smiling face. Immediately, I relaxed and settled in. I had a lot to think about, and despite what Holly thought of her, it seemed Arletta always said or did something to help untangle my thoughts.

The whole show was centered on the end of school and was filmed in an auditorium in Osage, Arkansas. During the audience participation section, a woman asked what were some of Arletta's ideas for teacher gifts. Another woman from the Osage PTA spoke about crafts that could make a difference, and Arletta posted a number for a charity that sold gently used band instruments that could be rented or purchased at a reduced price.

By the end of the show, my notebook lay open on the coffee table filled with notes and sketches. I always wrote direct quotes from Arletta in pen in my neatest cursive. Sometimes, I even went back after a show and shaded letters to make it look like calligraphy. I also recorded the best craft ideas step-by-step in pencil so I could add illustrations and my own personal touches.

> "The best gifts speak to the heart and don't need to come with a hefty price tag." —AP

1. "Thanks for Helping Me Grow" Flower Pot

Take a small clay pot and cover the lower section with chalkboard paint and paint the rim yellow. After the paint dries, use a permanent marker to make the yellow rim look like a ruler. Then write "Thanks for helping me grow" in chalk on the body of the pot.

2. Apple Jelly Jar

Use any small glass jar with a lid. Paint the jar red (it may take several coats) and the lid green. Glue on two green leaves cut from

card stock, add a wooden knob or even an
empty wooden spool to the top for a stem,
and then fill with your candy of choice (or
your teacher's favorite, if known).

3. Pencil Pencil Case

Clean a can from the recycling bin. Glue
pencils side-by-side to completely cover the
outside of the can. Fill with your teacher's
favorite markers or more pencils!

The show ideas sounded like good ones.
Nan's laptop lay on the coffee table, and I flipped
it open to use the store locator function on the
SmartMart website. I typed in Osage, Arkansas.
Holly was right; a SmartMart was already there
with a Superstore due to open soon.

Arletta might be the face of SmartMart, and
she may only be filming in these little towns
because of a store opening, but SmartMarts
would open with or without her. She'd been a
comfort to me for years, and I couldn't see her
as some sort of evil mastermind like everybody

else seemed to. But Holly, Abby, Colton, and even bossy old Miss Esther meant something to me too. Maybe something more.

I lowered my head into my hands, heard a rustling in the kitchen, and looked over to see Nan getting a glass of water. "How's my girl?" she asked.

"How do I figure out who's wrong when everyone seems right?" I asked.

She took a long drink. "In my experience, it's not often someone's all the way, top-to-bottom right. Or wrong either. 'Things aren't always simple, but most things worth doing aren't.'"

"Who said that?" I asked.

"That one is a Nan Johnson original with a dash of Teddy Roosevelt." Nan turned to go back to her room.

"Nan?" She stopped and faced me. I took a deep breath and said what I'd been scared to admit to myself. "This rally is important to me. But it's not going to be easy to pull off. The hard things have always been easier when I've had your help. I could use it now."

Nan smiled. "When you put it that way, sugar, how can I say no?" After giving me a kiss on the head, she carried the water back to her bedroom and left me to think. The more I thought, the more I kept coming back to one thing: Blessed, Alabama. When I'd finally told Nan about being called Donut Hole, instead of talking to my teacher or telling me to stand up for myself, she'd packed. We were settled in Oklahoma two days later.

That quote didn't have a smidge of Nan in it. Nan and I didn't do hard. Whenever times got the tiniest bit complicated, we did one thing. We moved.

HOPE SPRINGS RALLYPOPS

Level: Beginner

Supplies:

* 80-oz bag of Jolly Rancher candies* (using three candies per lollipop, one bag will make about 126 lollipops)

* Lollipop or popsicle sticks

* 4-inch by 6-inch clear candy bags

* Twine

* Gift tags

Tools:

* Aluminum foil

* 2 cookie sheets

* Nonstick cooking spray

* Select your candies to match a color theme! For example, use your school colors for pep rallies or other fundraisers.

Directions:

1. Preheat the oven to 275°F. Line two cookie sheets with aluminum foil and spray with nonstick cooking spray.

2. Place three candies in a cluster with the long sides almost touching (leave about ¼ inch between candies so they have room to spread as they melt). Use the same flavor for a solid lolly, or different flavors for a striped lolly. Be sure to leave room at the bottom of the sheet for the sticks.

3. Bake for 3 to 5 minutes, keeping a close eye on them. Once candies begin to melt and spread, remove from the oven. Don't wait until they bubble.

4. While candies are still hot, place the stick at one of the ends; gently press and twist so both sides of the stick are covered. Work quickly, before the candies harden.

5. When completely cool, place one lollypop per candy bag, tie with twine, and attach a gift tag.

Tip: Use only green apple candies, then dip them in melted caramel and let them rest on wax paper before packaging. It's extra effort, but you can charge twice as much! Sometimes, hard things are worth more, literally.

16

Give and Take

The Fabric Barn was the busiest I'd ever seen it, and I couldn't restock quilting supplies fast enough. A line five deep waited at the register while Holly finished reading the newspaper. She pointed to a page and yelled, "Our Jubilee is famous! She's front-page news!" Every head in the store turned to look at me. Heat rushed to my cheeks, and I considered sticking my head under a pile of cotton batting.

The local paper had run an article about the festival and an interview with Abby and me.

Despite our begging him to join, Colton opted out, claiming he didn't have anything to say. We'd huddled around the phone in Abby's mom's office for the conference call, fought off some serious giggles, and ended up answering the questions without sounding totally clueless. Also, Abby's mom announced a quilting contest in the article. The winner would collect a prize of five hundred dollars and the quilt would hang for a year in city hall.

Holly folded the paper and smacked it down on the counter. "A week's not nearly enough time for a good quilt. But for five hundred dollars, I'm dang sure going to try." The ladies buying upholstery fabric agreed and attacked my quilting display.

It seemed just the idea of Main Street Fest made people come to town to shop. Downtown was bustling. Seven whole cars kept the lonely traffic light company as they waited for green. It was a Hope Springs traffic jam.

Holly and I only had a few free moments after closing to set up the back room for her first class.

She'd rebraided her hair, spilled a box of thread, and after picking the spools up, had taken to pacing back and forth.

"What if I'm so rusty they get up and leave?" she asked.

"I'll block the doors," I said. "Speaking of, seems like there are three people already waiting to get in."

Before Holly went up front, she picked up the jar of rallypops and pulled one out. There were only two left, but we'd been so busy she hadn't had a chance to look at them. She took a second now to read one of the gift tags. LICK THE COMPETITION AND BUY LOCAL.

"These are perfect. You're a genius, sweetheart."

I blushed. Wynn and Nan had volunteered to deliver more than twenty jars of rallypops while I was working. For two full days we worked to make more than two hundred suckers. We listened—well, Nan and I listened while Wynn sang—to classic country music. We'd been a country-singing sucker-assembly line.

Last night, when Nan tied the twine on the two-hundredth sucker, she'd smiled at me. Her eyes shone as she looked at the pile of sweets we'd created. "This is really something. What you're doing...well, I've never seen anything like it. I'm happy you talked me into being part of it." Something inside me loosened a bit, like Nan's pride in me had melted away the tight nervousness I'd carried without knowing it was even there.

Wynn nodded. "Nothing like doing something good," he said and left the room. He returned wearing the apron I'd made him. He only nodded at me, and I couldn't think of a time I'd been happier. I smiled until my face ached.

The next morning, he had the apron on again and wore it all through dinner that evening. At first, I'd been glad that he'd changed his mind, but then again, it was also a constant reminder of Momma's unread letters. Part of me wondered if he'd really given in or gotten just what he wanted.

The past few days had been jam-packed with

Main Street Fest business. I'd cut and folded squares of fabric for the quilting class and tried to push away the thought of leaving, the box of letters under my bed, and Momma in general.

Abby's dad had the banner rushed, and it stretched across Main Street advertising the festival. I could see the bottom through the front windows of the Fabric Barn, and catching little glimpses of it settled my thoughts. Like the feeling my bike gave me, the banner reminded me of what I had now and all the people I cared about in Hope Springs.

Holly cleared her throat, "Well, guess I better let them in."

"You'll do great," I said. "And I'm here to do whatever you need." She stood straight, threw back her shoulders, and walked up front.

I greeted people and showed them to the back room. As much as I tried to focus on Holly's class, the maps lurked in the back of my mind. For Nan those maps meant fresh possibilities. But the more I thought about it, the more I thought there were plenty of possibilities right here in Hope Springs.

I just had to find the courage to tell Nan that. To persuade her to stay.

Then who should limp in but Nan herself. I almost felt like I'd summoned her and wouldn't have been any more surprised if she'd appeared in a puff of smoke like a genie from a lamp. There wasn't a single person I expected to see less at a quilting class than Nan.

"What are you doing here?" I asked.

"If that's your standard greeting, it needs work," she joked.

"Sorry, just surprised, that's all."

"Well, I feel like I hardly see you. You're either at Abby's or here. So I figured I'd come to you and see what you've been up to." She looked around. "This place is transformed. Did you do all this?"

"Some of it," I said.

Nan pointed to the signs I'd made. "Looks like more than some." She scanned the displays and racks. "I see your touch everywhere. You've made this a real home away from home." She smiled, but her voice was heavy, sad almost.

"Come, I'll help you into your seat."

"I can manage," she said. "But you may have to give me a hand when it comes to the actual crafting."

The class was for beginners, and Holly introduced the supplies and went over what she'd teach. She held up a tool that looked sort of like a round-bladed pizza slicer. "This is your rotary cutter. You'll use it, your quilting mat, and your quilter's ruler tonight to measure and cut the pieces for your first square. I'll also share some simple square patterns for you to choose from. Why don't you all take a minute to sort through the remnants on your table and chose about a half dozen that grab your eye."

I stood by Nan and was surprised by how much she chatted with the ladies next to her. She smiled up at me. "I've been cooped up for so long, I forgot what it was like to talk to anyone but Wynn. I can't tell you how happy I am to have him around again." She switched to a whisper. "But that man sings far too loud." I laughed, but we hushed when Holly cleared her throat.

Holly held up a seam ripper. "Now, we all know what this is. This little tool is magical and can alter the past and erase your mistakes." That got a laugh, and Holly settled into teaching. "But the thing is, a mistake can teach you a lot more than a perfect seam."

Nan nodded in agreement, and I wished I'd brought my notebook to jot down some Holly Paine quotes. Nan's selection of remnants was a little flashy for my tastes, but I figured she hadn't come to hear my advice. Just as I was about to break and suggest maybe not pairing purple with orange, the phone rang. I nodded at Holly and ran to the front.

"Fabric Barn. Jubilee speaking."

"What took you so long?" Abby asked.

"I was in the back."

"Arletta's people called Mom this morning."

I almost dropped the phone.

"Dad's been asked to cater the show, and they

want me to ask a question during something called the Audience Inclusion Segment." Abby said. "Get this. They *gave* me the question. Told me to memorize it before the show. Hardly live if it's scripted." She paused. "Jubilee?"

"Yes?"

"Did you hear me?" she asked

"Are you saying you get to talk to Arletta Paisley? Do you get to go up on stage with her?"

"No, I just ask—and I quote—'Fall is my favorite season, so I was wondering if you had some fun ideas for autumn-inspired crafts?' Who talks like that? They just want the mayor's kid on camera; the lady even said so. You can ask it, if you want."

My brain almost froze at the possibility of talking to Arletta. "Well, maybe they give kids the questions in case of nerves. They don't want you to stumble on live TV."

"It didn't seem that way to me. But either way, you can ask it."

"Oh. Okay. If you insist." I set the phone down to dance around and quietly squeal, realizing too late that I'd accidentally hung up without saying goodbye. I was going to ask Arletta Paisley a question! I did another dance, and then I called Abby back.

"Sorry," I said. "I got too excited. You sure?"

"Yep. You should do it. Besides, I've got to prepare for the Family Pairs tournament tomorrow. And I don't even like her. You do." Abby was quiet, and so was I.

"Well, okay. I'll talk to you later." I hung up, wishing I hadn't called back at all. Suspecting someone didn't like your TV momma was a lot different than hearing it said out loud.

LOCAL KIDS MAKE A BIG IMPACT

Three eleven-year-olds are responsible for expanding the annual Main Street Fest parade into a full-blown festival. The young activists are Hope Springs natives Colton Griggs and Abby Standridge, daughter of the mayor, and newcomer Jubilee Johnson. The kids have been hard at work promoting the event in hopes of rallying support for local businesses as the opening of the SmartMart Superstore nears.

"It was really Abby's idea, and we couldn't have done it without Colton and his dad offering up a venue. I just made some posters and the rallypops," Johnson said. The rallypops she refers to are treats free with a purchase at many Hope Springs local shops.

Yet, Standridge begs to differ. "The idea was totally Jubilee's. She thought a way to make everybody feel good would be to do something together," she said.

Though the girls can't agree on whose idea launched their efforts, they do agree on one thing: "Hope Springs is the best place I've ever lived," Johnson said.

"Me too," added Standridge.

They have the support of Mayor Myrna Standridge. "The kids are hoping to return Main Street Fest to what it once was—a celebration of our community. Following the annual parade, there'll be a rally at Griggs' Rigs Racing. The chamber of commerce is also sponsoring a quilt competition with a grand prize of five hundred dollars contributed by local businesses. The winner will be announced at the rally. I personally couldn't be more impressed by all the support and interest we've had so far. More events seem to be developing daily," Mayor Standridge added. "Just goes to show what even a small community such as ours can do when we unite behind a common cause."

The parade is scheduled to begin at 1 p.m. with the rally starting shortly after at 3 p.m. There will be booths selling goods from local stores and restaurants. A small stage is under construction for bands, and the quilting contest winner will be announced at 6 p.m.

_____

Go Fish

Wynn helped Nan into the passenger seat and even tried to fasten her seat belt, which earned him a smack on the hand.

"I'm not a child, Wynn," Nan said.

"All right, all right," Wynn said. "I know you only went to this class to get away from me."

Nan laughed. "I enjoyed it. It was fun to see Jubilee at work. You wouldn't believe what she's done in that store."

"I do believe it." Wynn smiled at me.

"Jubliee, you know I had my doubts about

this rally and you getting tangled up with all these people we hardly know. Worried you'd be disappointed or hurt." Nan cleared her throat just as we passed under the banner. "But now I think it might hurt worse not to see it through."

Nan hardly ever admitted she was wrong. I didn't know what to say but was saved when a huge tour bus pulled out in front of us making its way toward the library.

"Would you look at that?" Wynn said. "I've seen a lot of buses in my time, and that's a nice one."

Arletta's show was filming in the community center by the library in a few days, and the thought of it made me dizzy. Trucks and vans already covered the parking lot to set up the stage and equipment. We passed the tour bus as it turned into the community center. What if Arletta was in there? I felt light, almost weightless, like floating on water. Then I thought of my phone call with Abby and sank.

Nan caught my eye in the rearview mirror. "You're awfully quiet."

Given Nan's tendency to move us at the first

sign of trouble, I didn't want to tell her anything was wrong, but that conversation with Abby kept replaying in my head. I was willing to lose Hope Springs before I lost Abby. I needed advice, and I couldn't wait until I saw Holly again. So Nan and Wynn would have to do.

I told them the whole conversation word for word. "Maybe I made her mad. Or maybe she's nervous about the tournament." I said. Then I sat back and waited for Nan to quote one of our Relocation Rules or some artist.

But instead she said, "Someone once told me hard times are easier with support. You'll have to go to this fishing tournament and cheer her on, show her you care about her more than Arletta and that show."

"Dang, Nan," Wynn said. "That's good advice."

"Well, don't sound so shocked," Nan grumbled.

"The tournament is at Lake Trenton," Wynn said. "It starts at five o'clock in the morning, but the weigh-in is at three."

Nan and I both stared at Wynn.

"What? Frank and I chatted a bit at the One Stop the other night," he said with a shrug.

I worked the whole next morning on three signs— one for each of us—and handed them out right before we all piled into Nan's car that afternoon. Lake Trenton was a twenty-minute drive filled with Wynn's singing and Nan and I exchanging eye rolls until we were both giggling. The more we laughed, the louder Wynn sang.

We pulled into an almost-full parking lot in front of a marina. People milled about between stands selling fishing gear and food. Nan, Wynn, and I wandered around until boats started to come in from the lake and people began to move toward a covered grandstand. I noticed signs advertising Main Street Fest and our rally posted all over. Abby must have come early and worked hard before the tournament started. I hadn't even thought to offer my help, and she hadn't asked for it.

The crowd cheered when a man with a bull-horn took the stage. After he welcomed everyone and thanked a long list of sponsors and volunteers, he announced the first team. Each catch was weighed, and names were posted on a leaderboard. We had to wait quite a while before Abby and her dad were called up to have their catches measured. As soon as their names were announced, Wynn and I whooped and hollered and waved our signs high. Nan did her best too. We caused such a fuss that people stared.

Abby's poof of hair was smashed under a ballcap and when she saw us, she buried her face in her hands. At first, I thought she was only embarrassed, but then she looked up, smiled, shook her head, and covered her face again.

They weighed Abby's catches. Five in all. The last fish drew some oohs and aahs. Seven pounds and nine ounces didn't sound like a lot to me, but what did I know? Abby and her dad were written up on the leaderboard.

We had to wait more than an hour for twenty-two teams to weigh in, but no one knocked Abby out of the top spot.

After the cash prizes and trophies were handed out, the announcer addressed the crowd and said, "Now, everybody here fished their hardest today. But only one fish can be the biggest, which is why every year we give out the Lake Trenton Hawg Award." He held up a shiny trophy, and the crowd broke out in rowdy applause.

"This year it was close, but Abby Standridge, come on up and collect this trophy and maybe the biggest prize of the tournament—bragging rights!"

Abby grabbed her hat with both hands and did a little jump. I smiled for her until my face ached. After she walked out and accepted the trophy, she took a minute to look it over before she held it up above her head. The crowd clapped, but Wynn, Nan, and I went wild. I noticed Abby's mom in the front row taking pictures.

When the excitement died down, Abby skipped over to me carrying her trophy. "Hey, I didn't know you guys were coming. I liked your sign."

I handed over the poster I'd spent the most time on, a big bass with red lips, eyelashes, and a crown covered in glitter and stick-on jewels. "Keep it." I nodded to Nan and Wynn. "And consider us your first fan club."

Abby's dad shook hands with Wynn and thanked Nan for coming while Abby gave me a hug. "I caught the biggest fish," she whispered. "It wasn't quite a lunker but it was close."

"I don't know what a lunker is," I whispered back, "but I'm proud of you."

Abby laughed. "Hey, want to go get a candy apple and a funnel cake and help me celebrate? Colton and his dad are around here somewhere. Mom's searching for a free table."

"A place to sit sounds like heaven," Nan said.

"We'll find Myrna and the boys, and you two meet us there," Abby's dad suggested.

Abby and I found a food truck, got in line, and she launched into a heated retelling of all her catches. "There's a five-catch limit. So, every time you get a bigger fish you cull your live well, meaning you throw the smallest fish back and let the bigger one take its place. By ten o'clock we still hadn't had much luck. Then dad snagged a hefty four-pounder. But we only caught peanuts after that, and by noon the fish get lazy and hunker down. I was desperate. So, I did the only thing I could think of."

"Used your stink bait?" I asked.

Abby nodded. "Dip bait, but yes. It works best on catfish, but I thought why not give it a try. I took a jig and coated it in the stuff. Dad thought it'd just dissolve in the water. But I managed to hit a mat, and I mean, as soon as that jig touched water, I got a bite. I could tell right away she was a whopper by the way she pulled."

I smiled and nodded along.

"Know what I mean?" she asked.

"Sort of," I said. "Not really."

She laughed and gently kicked the pavement with her sneaker. "I'm surprised you came."

"I know. I've been too wrapped up in Arletta and the live show. But I wanted to tell you something." I paused, so used to telling half lies that I could hardly get the truth to come out. "My dad passed when I was little. Wynn isn't just a family friend. I mean, he is, but he was my dad's best friend and is still close with my mom. She sent him to stay with us when Nan got hurt because she couldn't be bothered to stay herself. My mom isn't all that...involved. Usually. I guess what I'm saying is, I'm not used to having a lot of people I can count on." It wasn't the whole truth, but it was as much as I could manage.

"I'm sorry, Jubilee." Abby bumped me with her shoulder. "But thank you for telling me and thank you for coming today."

"That's what friends are for, right?" I asked.

"Right." Abby put an arm over my shoulder. "We can count on each other."

Abby and I got our food then headed to the picnic area. The first person I saw was Colton standing and waving both arms next to two tables where everyone else sat.

I could tell Abby the rest, about Momma wanting me back, another time. For now, I'd enjoy the hot sun, a freshly fried funnel cake, and the warm feeling of having a friend and a whole lot of people to count on.

18

Needing to Know

The next morning, I planned and changed outfits at least a dozen times. Suddenly nothing I owned seemed right for Arletta Paisley's live show. No matter what I put on, it felt backward, inside out, and two sizes too small. Abby's mom pulled up in their minivan, and I fought the urge to dash back to my room and change one last time.

"You look perfect," Nan said.

"Just remember, everyone's watching *her*, not you. Even though you're much more interesting in my opinion," Wynn said. "Also, people always say to picture everyone naked when you're nervous. But that's a terrible idea, makes your whole face curl up. I say picture everyone wearing clown wigs and fanny packs."

Nan shook her head, stood, looked me over, and put her hands on my shoulders. "Courage is 'grace under pressure.' Ernest Hemingway." I wasn't so sure what that one meant, but then she gave me one of her rare hugs. "You've got nothing to be nervous about. You are all grace." She walked me to the door, and they both watched and waved longer than necessary.

Abby sat up front and Colton slid the door open for me from the back seat. He looked like he always did, which was perfect.

My nerves jittered so much it felt like my skin was giving off electricity. It would be a wonder if my hair wasn't standing on end by the time we got there. Everyone chatted for the short drive, except me. I didn't say a single word, like if I sat quiet and still enough, I wouldn't explode.

Inside the community center, Hearth & Home people shuffled back and forth everywhere. Some wore headsets, but others sat in the audience with earpieces like the undercover secret service. Our seats were three rows from the front, and I scanned the audience, only noticing a few familiar faces, the *Queen of Neat* theme song playing quietly in the background.

Abby leaned into me and whispered, "I don't think half these people even live in Hope Springs."

I hardly heard her; that theme song synced up with my pounding heartbeat. It was my national anthem, and I was about to meet the queen.

Arletta Paisley appeared at the very last minute; signs flashed for applause. I clapped until my hands stung. She wore cowboy boots with a long white ruffled skirt and a denim shirt and waved like a beauty queen—a perfect combination of folksy and classy. A cameraman held his hand high and counted down from three.

The lump in my throat was the size of a full ball of yarn.

Arletta laughed her wind-chime laugh and said, "Here we are, folks. In my hometown of Hope Springs. I can't tell y'all how good it feels to be back!"

Abby rolled her eyes, Colton crossed his arms, the sign flashed, and the audience cheered. The show went by like a dream. Arletta Paisley started with her intro. Then the Hope Springs middle school principal talked about the problem with bake sales: promoting healthy food choices versus the importance of student-led fundraising. He and Arletta made some healthy treats together that could be sold along with braided key chains and bracelets in school colors. The signs for applause flashed again, and we went to commercial break.

Abby and Colton whispered about the festival, but my eyes were glued to the stage where Arletta Paisley sat with a herd of Hearth & Home employees fluttering around her like the birds and mice in Cinderella, refreshing her makeup, fluffing her hair—one even buffed her boots with a white cloth napkin. A girl who looked a little older than me carried out a plate piled high with a signature Frank burger and fries from the One Stop. Arletta Paisley took one look at it, cupped her hand over the microphone hidden in the fold of her blouse, and said just loud enough for someone really listening and watching her lips to make out, "I can't eat that crap. Bring me a cup of hot tea with a wedge of lemon."

Before too long the camera came back on and so did Arletta's signature smile. The next section was the one I'd been waiting for. An audience member asked a prepared question, and Arletta Paisley gave a natural but also prepared answer. Every time the camera was off Arletta, her smile disappeared. With each cut to commercial, I worried more and more that my Arletta wasn't who I thought she was.

When it was Abby's turn, she held the microphone and waited. I started to whisper "Row, Row, Row Your Boat" and, with her free hand, Abby grabbed mine and squeezed.

I'd memorized her question, practiced with

Nan and Wynn for about an hour, and could recite it as easy as I could my own name. When the camera panned over to us, Abby passed the mic to me, and I stood. The Hearth & Home employees went ballistic and swung their arms like they were waving in a jumbo jet.

And I froze. I just stood there with my mouth hanging open. Then I saw Arletta Paisley—I mean really *saw* her. She rolled her eyes, whispered something to someone off stage, and shook her head. Then she pulled on a smile like a roman shade rolling up, motioned at me, and then mouthed the words "You're on."

"Hi, Arletta. I'm Jubilee Johnson. I've been a fan of yours for—well, about forever," I said. The audience laughed.

Arletta Paisley didn't miss a beat. "What a sweet name, Jubilee. Do people call you Jubi for short?"

"Some people do," I answered.

She beamed and nodded for me to go ahead. "And you have something you want to ask? Let's hear it, sweetheart."

Abby's question was stuck somewhere between my brain and my mouth, so instead, I asked what I needed to know.

"I'm wondering how you feel about Smart-Mart building a Superstore just down the highway. A lot of people in Hope Springs are scared it'll cause local business to suffer."

The audience murmured, and Arletta sat there and blinked and smiled for a few seconds too long. She recovered quickly, though, and out came that wind-chime laugh, a little strained this time. "Well, Jubilee Johnson, that's a good question. Change can be scary, but I can assure you SmartMart doesn't mean any harm to Hope Springs. I personally plan on doing some shopping downtown today right after the show." The applause sign flashed, Arletta laughed, the audience clapped, and she moved on. She answered the other questions flawlessly. It was minutes before I could breathe like a normal person.

Abby leaned over to me. "Why didn't you tell me you were going to do that?"

"I didn't know it myself until it happened," I said.

She shook her head and smiled.

"Now, that was something," Colton said. It was only four words, but I played them over and over in my head and almost missed the whole segment on school-wide fundraisers for charities.

During the next commercial break, a Hearth & Home employee with a grubby goatee approached our aisle and pointed at me. "Ms. Paisley would like to see you after the show," he said.

I hesitated, and Colton said, "We'll all go."

The man shook his head. "Only Jubilee Johnson." He gave us a tight-lipped smile and walked away.

I knew Arletta might be miffed over my question, but she was my idol. I wasn't ready to give her up altogether. Besides, maybe she was just having a bad day. Bad days could set even the most wonderful person's mood crooked. Heck, they often sent Nan and me packing.

The rest of the show went by without a hitch.

When it was over, the same goateed guy showed Abby and Colton to a bench backstage. I kept picturing him wearing a clown wig and fanny pack, but it wasn't helping much. He walked me to an emergency exit and pointed to a fancy RV parked across five spaces in the roped-off parking lot, the same tour bus from Main Street. A gold glittery star bearing Arletta's name in looping fuchsia cursive sparkled on the door.

I tripped up the two steps in a daze, my heart beating so hard I could feel it in my ears. I knocked and jumped when a woman with a long ponytail opened the door.

Arletta sat in an overstuffed armchair covered in a country rose pattern. I pasted on a smile and hoped she couldn't hear my pulse hammering. She smiled back and the other woman gave me a worried glance before leaving and closing the door behind her.

Then it was just the two of us.

Me and Arletta Paisley. My Arletta. My TV momma. With me through every move and in every new place.

"Jubilee Johnson," she said. She held out her hand, not for me to shake, but in front of her face, examining her nails. She flicked one, and her smile vanished. "Who sent you?"

"What?" I asked.

She narrowed her eyes. "Was it Martha's people? She's been after my audience for years."

"Nobody sent me. I just moved here. I work at the Fabric Barn with Holly Paine," I stammered. "She went to high school with you. Hope Springs High." I made myself stop talking and bit down nervous laughter.

"Holly Paine. Oh, I remember her. Mousy little thing. Does she still wear her hair in that awful braid?" Arletta asked.

Then she laughed like we were old friends gossiping.

"Let me tell you a little secret, Jubilee. If you have any sense, you'll get out of this town. I left as fast as I could, and look at me now." She did a little ta-da motion. "I heard all about this rally some kids whipped up. I'm guessing that's you and your friends. But what if I offered you a top-of-the-line Crock-pot or a new bedspread or a whole room makeover?"

I didn't answer. And Holly wasn't mousy. She was dedicated and generous and kind. With each good quality I could name, my brow furrowed deeper. And what in the world would I do with a Crock-pot?

"Hmm. What about another chance to be on the show? All of America would forget about you standing there like a deer in headlights." She paused to act out an impression of me, eyes wide and mouth hanging open. "Then you and I can just forget all this rally nonsense."

Each word she spoke chipped away at what I'd thought of her. Then I finally saw it, what Abby and Holly Paine had seen all along. Arletta Paisley was a phony. From her gel-tipped fingernails to the ends of her glued-on eyelashes. All the way through and back again, a fake. She was trying to bribe me, buy me off so I'd back out of the rally. I bit my tongue and crossed my arms.

When I didn't answer, her smile disappeared, and she stared at me colder and harder by the second. "Oh well. I tried to make friends with you, Jubilee, but it doesn't really matter in the long run. I mean, I'm me and you're just a kid, after all. Be sure to tell my old friend Holly to read the paper this week."

I'd pushed away or justified every piece of evidence that Arletta was a phony. Like a little kid believed in fairies or princesses, I'd believed in Arletta. I'd not only been childish, but foolish too. I stood there feeling more like a donut hole than all the times I'd been called one.

"Well, go on," Arletta said. "Shoo." And she actually did a little skedaddle motion with her hands like I was a stray cat.

I backed away but stopped with one foot out the door. "You know, I've moved a lot and never really met a place I didn't mind leaving until I moved here. Maybe you should think about whether there's something wrong with Hope Springs or with you. Now, after having met you,

I know what I think." Then I turned and left without giving her a backward glance.

As soon as I got back to the hallway, Abby and Colton ran up to me.

"Are you all right?" Abby asked. At first, I couldn't answer. *Was* I all right?

Colton grabbed my hand. "What happened?" His fingers around mine felt like being struck by lightning. That jolt was exactly what I needed.

I looked back and forth between them, their faces all serious with concern. Concern for me. They were my friends, real through and through. One of Nan's favorite quotes from that Hemingway guy floated back to me, the inspiration for Relocation Rule Number 17. "Now is no time to think of what you do not have. Think of what you can do with what there is." Maybe some of the Relocation Rules were still worth something after all. Hope Springs had given me more than I'd ever had.

"We're going to need reinforcements," I said.

"We've already called everybody in town about the rally," Abby said.

"I have someone else in mind."

"Like who?" Colton let go of my hand, but I hardly noticed.

My mind was two-stepping around a plan. "You two ever heard of a country singer named Lexie Kirk?"

19

A Place to Sing

Moving every six to nine months had made me an expert at doing new things. I still got nervous, but after a while, the stomach-twisting nerves that went along with the unknown turned into only a flutter. But calling Momma and saying a few unfamiliar words had my heart feeling like it was stretched across Holly's quilting frame.

After my slap-in-the-face meeting with Arletta, I was out of sorts and doubting most of my hard-held truths. Our Relocation Rules had more holes than fishnet. But one thing I'd clung to longer and harder than Arletta being the best thing since hot glue was that Momma was unforgivable.

As soon as I walked through the door, Nan asked how it'd gone. "Well, I learned Arletta isn't who she pretends to be."

"Few of us are," she said. "You want to talk about it? There's something I need to run by you too."

"Sure," I said. "I just need to do some things first." I walked back to my room, trying to hold on to some of the determination I'd felt earlier.

Momma's letters started off with pale pink envelopes that increased in intensity over the years to a bright fuchsia. When I slid one out, my hands shook. The pages quivered so much, I had to rest them on my bed to keep the handwriting of Momma's first letter from wiggling away from me.

Jubilee,

There is something magical about singing, something transformative. I read once that music can change us. When I sing, I'm not a wreck or a widow. When I sing, I'm something better than myself. Maybe that's why I love it so much, because I get to escape being me and get to forget for a little while.

Only two things have ever come close to giving me that same feeling. That's your daddy and you. Never in my life have I felt so lifted up and more than myself than when I met you for the first time. That's why we named you Jubilee. It means a season of celebration, and that's how me and your daddy felt, like dancing and raising our hands up thanking God for giving us you.

In the hospital, I held you and thought there had never been anything so perfect.

The truth is, your daddy was better than me. I pray every day that you end up with more pieces of him than me. I pray that you are strong but forgiving, that you are resilient but hopeful, and that you are kind but nobody's fool. Though I didn't have much to do with it, it makes me proud to see those things in you already.

There's a part of me that knows you'll be the best thing I ever do.

You're not going to remember your daddy,
and it hurts me to think about that. But maybe
it's better that way, because remembering him
and being without him was truly killing me. I
know it's not reasonable to think you'll forgive me,
but I hope you don't let my leaving hurt you too
much for too long. Yes, I knew it would hurt, but
I also knew I was capable of hurting you worse
if I stayed. Nan raised your daddy, and I hate
to admit it, but she'll do a better job than I ever
could.

Being a singer has always been my dream,
and I know I'm a much better singer than I am a
mother. But that isn't the reason I left you with
Nan.

I didn't do it so I could sing, I did it so you
could.

I love you still and always will,
Your Momma

It took me a few hours, but I read every letter. Almost a whole box of tissues lay wadded
up from crying over her words. But my feelings

for Momma didn't work like a light switch; they were all tangled, one on top of the other. A nest of anger and hurt knotted up inside me, and I felt that loosen a little—not all the way, but a little.

After I'd calmed down, I called. When she answered, I didn't even say hello. I took a deep breath and said, "Momma, I need your help."

Her first word was yes, then she cried for ages. One thing I'd forgotten when I realized Momma might give us the upper hand against Arletta and SmartMart was that she was still Momma. But she didn't make it about her this time.

"What can I do?" she asked. I told her almost everything, and we worked out a plan. Turned out Momma was good at planning too. Before we hung up, she said, "I'll help, but I might be able to recruit one more person who could make an even bigger difference."

After that call, I was too excited to sit for dinner.

"You're awful riled up," Nan said. "Need any help?"

"I think I've got it about figured out. There are a few details to get sorted, though." I filled both Nan and Wynn in. Nan nodded and offered to call the businesses that hadn't yet agreed to participate in the festival. Wynn was quick to pull out his phone and call Momma to discuss the concert details.

"I've got a couple of calls to make too." I started toward my bedroom.

"Maybe we can talk later?" Nan asked. "There are a few things I could use some help figuring out."

"Sure," I said, ignoring the worry in her tone. Nothing bad could happen. Not now when I'd almost solved all my problems.

My fingers shook when I dialed Colton's number.

"How big is the stage you're building?"

"Big enough for about five people sitting in chairs," he answered.

"What if I told you I could get my momma and maybe Brent Chisholm too?" I asked.

"I'd say we need a bigger stage."

The very next day, Brent Chisholm sat for an interview on *The Country Call,* a Dallas morning news show, and announced his free impromptu concert in Hope Springs—a chance to show his support for local small businesses across the heartland. The broadcast gained national news coverage. All my plans seemed to be fitting together like the teeth on a zipper, and I forgot all about the few things Nan needed help figuring out.

20

Happily Ever After

The smell of Wynn cooking up a heap of bacon and eggs wafted through the air when I entered the kitchen. I was just about to greet him but stopped dead in my tracks. Nan sat at the table and so did my Arletta Paisley® linen expandable snap-top folder in robin's-egg blue with a matching damask liner.

The maps were out for breakfast.

"I give up. What's in the box?" Wynn asked.

"Well, Jubilee and I have a family tradition of picking out new towns together. These are

all our maps, but I guess we only need the one
of Texas this time. I'm due to start at the nursing home here soon, so we have some decisions
to make. Dallas might work or we could move
back to Arkansas. I say Dallas. I'm always up
for a change of scenery. 'The measure of intelli-
gence is the ability to change.' Albert Einstein."
Then she gulped down the last of her coffee and
slammed the mug on the table like that was that.
Seemed she'd figured everything out without me.

"Well, it seems like this solution works for you
and Lexie. But what about what Jubilee wants?
You know she's settled in here. Besides that, Nan,
a change for you would be to stay in one place."

I eyed him. He'd stopped what he was doing
and was staring at Nan. She glared right back.
He was tiptoeing up to what I didn't dare do—
disagree with Nan.

"I don't see how it's your business, Wynn, but
if you must know, Alexandra called and she's
forcing my hand. These are the only two options
I could get her to agree to. She likes the idea of
Jubilee going back to the same school and having

some *consistency*, but she likes the idea of Jubilee being closer even better. I figured you'd know all about it, being her right-hand man."

"No, I…Lexie hasn't talked to me much about her decisions lately. But I'll call her today if that would make a difference." I noticed his mouth shut in a hard line, and Nan clenched her fork. I'd never fought Nan on a move before. In fact, I'd never fought much for anything before. They both turned to me, and I fell back on the only way I'd learned to handle big problems—I made a dash for the door and left.

The walk to the pond was different on my own. Quieter, for one. I'd never noticed the way the tall pasture grass bent with the wind. I yanked up a handful and threw it on the path, then stomped on it for good measure. I'd been wrong about Arletta, maybe wrong about Momma too. Maybe I was wrong about everything, Hope Springs included. Believing in perfect places was as stupid as believing in unicorns, or that a TV personality was a good substitute for a real momma.

No sooner had I sat down on a stump than

I heard someone huffing and grunting up the path. I stood and saw Nan limping along, already red in the face from the effort. When she finally reached me, she said, "Scoot over so I can sit with you for a minute."

I scooted but stared straight ahead. We sat in silence. She didn't say anything, and I already felt the tightness of a good cry building in my throat.

"You remember when you were little, you'd come up with the wildest outfits? You'd pull my knee-high hose on your hands like evening gloves. Even wore a purse on your head like a hat for a full month. You were always so creative."

I fixed my eyes on the still surface of the pond.

"Wynn said this place reminds him of Tullahoma. He's right. That's where your dad met your mom. Not long after, you came along. They were so young, so we stayed there longer than we'd ever stayed anywhere before. Even bought a piano."

A piano was not packable. A piano was meant to stay in one place.

"The thing is, with all this moving, I've put us in a risky spot. If your Momma involves an attorney...well, a judge might lean to her side. She's more than hinted at wanting you back. Thinks I'm too irresponsible."

"She's one to talk," I mumbled.

Nan held a hand up to stop me from saying more. "And if I'm honest, she has a point. Surely, we can find a place closer to Dallas that'll do. That way, she can feel more involved. Or we can go back. Start you up at the same school. Show her I'm serious about changing my ways. I settled down once before for your dad. I'd happily do it again rather than risk losing you."

Everything I'd kept inside seemed to knot up and work its way into my throat, like I needed to scream to get it out. I figured yelling at Nan might make me feel better for a minute, but I'd feel even worse later on. We were a team, like those kissing squirrel salt and pepper shakers. One without the other, and you'd just have a lonely squirrel reaching out for something that wasn't there.

I did remember wearing a purse on my head. And Nan went with it, taking me to the grocery store and daycare with my handbag hat, smiling the whole time. I didn't remember Momma there at all.

Nan set her hand on mine; her veins ran a pale blue like the rivers on one of our maps. She squeezed, and I squeezed back. I wasn't sure of much anymore, but I was sure I belonged with her.

"I like it here." I looked out over the pond again and thought of Abby and Colton. "Maybe we could…" One word: *stay*, and I couldn't say it. The idea of Arkansas and Mr. Taft and that dingy apartment was twisting my heart like a wet dishrag, but why let her know how much this move would hurt if it was our only option, our only way to stay together? I fought down the knot in my throat to talk. "Maybe we could wait until after Main Street Fest. Since I've already worked so hard on it."

"Sure, honey. School doesn't start for a few months, so we've got a little time to wrap things up," she said. "What do you say we walk back together? I'm not sure I can make it on my own."

With Nan's arm over my shoulder we lumbered along, and I felt like I was leaving a bread crumb trail of my heart the whole way back. When we reached our rental, a *Hope Springs Gazette* lay on our front step. The headline caught my eye as I helped Nan in and Wynn said, "Made a fresh pot of coffee."

Coffee was a grown-up peace offering. Nan nodded and patted him on the forearm. I sat at the kitchen table and unfolded the paper. Any doubt that Arletta wasn't what she pretended to be on TV disappeared as I read the article. Holly was right—pretty dang close to all the way, top-to-bottom right.

SMARTMART AND PAISLEY: HAPPILY EVER AFTER

SmartMart already has an exclusive Arletta Paisley® line of housewares, a deal that reportedly led to Paisley's recent role as SmartMart's spokeswoman. But now the two move from partnership to marriage with the announcement that Paisley will have her own department in each Superstore, called Paisley Notions—dedicated primarily to sewing and other crafts.

The new department was revealed at SmartMart's flagship store in Dallas earlier in the week. Large flat-screen TVs play reruns of Paisley's Hearth & Home Network show, *Queen of Neat*. Also available are episode-specific craft packages, a line of print fabrics designed by Paisley, and a weekly class focusing on a craft from the show.

"I couldn't be more excited. Anyone who watches my shows knows that I believe crafting can change lives. SmartMart is giving me an even bigger opportunity to do just that," Paisley said.

21

That Hemingway Guy

I t's top-of-the-line. Computerized. Can sew denim, leather, probably Sheetrock too. Self-threading, with a top-loading bobbin, and a free swing arm for more creativity. It's the Swiss Army knife of sewing machines." Holly switched to a whisper. "And I love it almost as much as I love Rayburn." Holly Paine's new sewing machine was gleaming white and covered with buttons.

"It's nice." I went back to sorting through old bolts of fabric. I was cutting and bundling quilting squares into a dozen fat quarters, a mix-and-matched stack of fabrics all measured and ready to sew. I'd decided to make a window display called "A Quilter's Dozen." With the deadline for the contest closing in, Holly was selling more quilting supplies than anything else.

"Nice?" Holly asked. "That's all you've got?" She sidled up to me. "I might even let you use it." She bumped me with her hip. "I'm going to win that contest for sure now that I've got this puppy to do the finishing touches. Entries are due in two days. So, there's not much time to get the border finished and whip the whole thing together. Come on, Rayburn, let's go set up."

She danced over to a sewing table. Rayburn didn't move from his dog bed—not even a wrinkle wiggled.

The newspaper was folded by the register with the Arletta article face up. Holly whistled while she plugged in the machine.

I couldn't take it anymore. "Why are you so happy? Did you read the article? She's basically putting a Fabric Barn in the SmartMart."

"Nothing like winning a fight when it seems like you're in for a real licking. Something for your lollipops." Holly laughed. I didn't.

"How can you not be worried? It feels like there's nothing we can do to beat her."

"Listen, honey. I'm not sure it's about beating her. If people around here want me to stay open, they'll keep shopping here. If they don't, well then, I'll figure something out. But don't give up hope. Business is better than it's been in years." Holly walked back over to me and made a point of looking me in the eye. "You and your friends have been such busy beavers. A single beaver can take down a whole tree. A few working together can change the flow of water. That's not nothing. What's got *you* so defeated all of a sudden?"

"We're thinking about moving again," I said.

"So soon?" she asked.

I nodded and focused on the fabric. *Measure, cut, count, stack, tie.* If I kept counting and tying, maybe I could push Momma and Wynn and Nan and losing most everything I cared about out of my mind and make it through the day without crying in front of Holly.

"Do you want to move, Jubilee?"

I shook my head.

"Have you told her that you want to stay?"

"Not exactly, but it's not that simple." Holly meant I should talk to Nan. She was right, but the person I really needed to have a talk with was Momma. All my life, I'd been angry at her for not taking an interest, not acting like a real momma. Now that she was doing what I'd wished for, I couldn't tell her living with her made as much sense to me as high-heeled sneakers.

"There's your problem, honey. Same thing happened to Claire Von Montclair and the General—she couldn't be honest about her feelings, so he left never knowing how deeply she loved him. And her lapse of courage cost her the love of a lifetime." Holly paused to stare off into the distance for a second. "If Nan's guessing about how you feel, she's got a fifty percent chance of guessing wrong. I don't know Nan well, but seems like she loves you and she'd listen. At least that part is simple." She put her hand on one of the bundles I'd tied. "Besides, you can't leave. You're the brains behind this operation."

Before I rode home, I took a walk over to the well in front of city hall and read the plaque again.

THIS WELL IS DEDICATED TO THE COURAGEOUS PIONEERS WHO SETTLED THIS TOWN IN THE YEAR 1836. DESPITE SEEMINGLY INSURMOUNTABLE HARDSHIP, INCLUDING THE DEVASTATING DROUGHT OF 1840, THESE BRAVE INDIVIDUALS RISKED THEIR LIVES TO LAY THE FOUNDATION FOR THE COMMUNITY THAT EXISTS TODAY. THEIR TIRELESS EFFORTS IN THE FACE OF ADVERSITY HAVE GIVEN US ALL A TREASURE WORTH MORE THAN GOLD—A HOME. WHILE THE SPRING IS NO MORE, LET THIS WELL BE A REMINDER THAT HOPE SPRINGS ETERNAL.

I took out a penny, made a wish, and tossed it. I didn't wish to change the past. Why waste a perfectly good penny? Besides, I'd decided with a large dose of the whole truth, a little courage, and some creativity, I might be able to change my present and maybe even my future. But a wish sure couldn't hurt.

That night after dinner, I asked Wynn to

excuse us. Nan raised her eyebrows at me as Wynn left, announcing it was a nice night for a solo walk.

Nan sat at our small kitchen table. "Just a sec. I've got to get something," I said. She smiled. I left and brought out my box of Momma's letters. Nan's smile disappeared—she'd been expecting the maps.

I handed Nan the first letter I'd opened.

Her eyes scanned the page. When she'd finished, I said, "I don't want to move." I slid the whole box of letters across the table to her. "I've been carrying these around with me, unopened, for years, ignoring how Momma felt and what she had to say because I was scared of how that'd make me feel. But since we've been here, I've realized something. 'You can't get away from yourself by moving from one place to another.' Ernest Hemingway, *The Sun Also Rises*." Prepping for this moment, it hadn't hurt to research famous author quotes; I knew I'd picked the right one.

Nan's brow wrinkled, her eyes filled, and the corners of her mouth dipped. Seeing her face crumple like that reminded me I wasn't the only one who'd been left behind. When Daddy died, he'd left Nan too. Starting on our first day in town I'd been letting go of our way of life bit by bit, and here I was asking Nan to let go all at once.

I pointed to the letter she still held. "I think I need to remind Momma of what she wrote in that letter. I'm different here, but not because I escaped being me, like Momma says. It's because I figured out more of who I am. I'm more me here, and I want to stay. If you gave Hope Springs a chance and we make this place our home, maybe you could be more you too."

Nan stood and wrapped me up in a hug even though I could tell it hurt. "I'll call your mom tonight and make another try at smoothing things out. A heart-to-heart between me and your momma is long overdue. And then I think we should all sit down and talk when she's here for the concert." All the nerves and guilt and fear that'd been building and sitting heavy as a boulder fell away. She wiped at a tear I'd let escape, pulled me in for another hug, and said, "We'll sort it out. Together this time."

22

A Perfect Match

The next morning, Nan and Wynn were up and eating breakfast while I dashed around getting ready. I'd overslept and was eager to rush to the Fabric Barn to finish my quilting window display. In the middle of the night, I'd had a vision of the window framed in poster board stitched with super-bulky yarn like the edge of a quilting square.

I was nearly out the door when Wynn said, "Hold up, Jubilee. I'd like to talk to you and Nan for a minute." Nan and I exchanged a look.

We settled around the kitchen table, and Wynn cleared his throat. "Your mother's career is taking off, and she's letting Brent's people manage it now. Things have been changing for a while, and there've been some...developments. Anyway, I spoke to her, told her what I thought." He took his eyes off his boots long enough to look at us. "I wondered if I could stay here a few more weeks while I figure out what's next for me. If the two of you could stand me for a bit longer, I'd appreciate it."

"Of course, Wynn," Nan said. "Besides, you've got to finish this kitchen. If we're here for a while, I'd sure like to eat without looking at those dag-blasted pink cabinets."

I nodded. *Here for a while.* Me and Nan and Wynn too. I looked up at our popcorn ceiling, closed my eyes, and took in a quivery breath. Could it be that everything would work out? Momma's dream was coming true. Maybe mine would too.

If Momma thought what was missing from her life was me, then I was open to the idea of giving her a second chance. But I'd rather give out my second chances from the place that taught me how to give them—Hope Springs.

Now, all that was left was to persuade her that staying with Nan and Wynn was what was best for me, despite what she wanted. Admitting my feelings to Nan was a bit different from telling Momma. For one, deep down, I figured Nan would put what I wanted first or at least consider it important. But Momma? For most of my life, I'd believed she only put herself first. But recently, it seemed the truths I'd clung to the hardest were the ones I needed to let go of the most.

Wynn forced a smile and a slice of toast on me before I could leave for the Fabric Barn. I was up and on my way out when he added, "Abby phoned while you were getting ready to ask if you'd stop by on your way."

"Okay." I paused. "Wynn, I'm sorry things didn't work out the way you wanted with Momma, but I'm glad you're staying."

"I've never been good at picking what was

best for me. But maybe this time, what was best for me happened without my having much to do with it." He gave me his first real smile of the morning. "Go on. Don't want to make you late."

On the ride to Abby's, I stopped on the side of the road just to listen and take a deep breath. There might not be perfect places, but Hope Springs was close. I resisted the urge to throw my arms out and spin in a wide circle, *Sound of Music* style.

As I pulled into Abby's driveway, she burst out the door, jumped down the steps of her porch, and ran to meet me. I could tell from her face she was in no mood for spinning.

"Arletta's people called Mom's office this morning. They'd like to show their support for Hope Springs and make what Mom called a 'significant donation' to the Downtown Revitalization Fund. But get this—on the condition that Arletta is given time to make a statement and introduce Brent Chisholm at the concert." She stepped from the drive into her yard, plopped right down on the grass, and held up her hands.

"Mom's got to give them an answer soon. I don't think she can afford to turn down that much money. And once Arletta's up there, she could say anything."

I helped her up and gave her a quick hug. Then I held her out from me and spun her around until we toppled over into the grass.

Abby laughed. "I think all those marshmallows are finally having an impact."

"Maybe so." I looked up at the new blue sky, bumped her sneaker with mine, and said, "Let her talk. Nothing Arletta Paisley can say could ruin anything."

I hopped on my bike, waving to Abby before I took off toward the Fabric Barn. This place was my perfect match, and I'd had enough of running the other way when life got messy.

Holly sat at the desk deep-reading another romance novel, *My General Returns*. In front of the cutting table sat three five-gallon buckets full of scraps.

"Got some more remnants for you to sort," she said without looking up, pointing to the buckets.

It was going to be a long day.

"Make piles of similar colors. Doesn't have to be perfect." She still didn't lift her eyes from the page but gasped, pressed a hand to her chest, and said, "I'll be right with you." She turned a page and whispered, "Well, me, oh my."

I made piles of light, dark, and bright fabrics and one pile I thought was too ugly for keeping. After a while, Holly came over.

"What's this?" she asked, pointing to my throwaway pile.

"I thought those were too bleh."

"Bleh?" she mumbled and pulled a sour face as she turned and headed to the back of the store. It took a couple of trips, but she ended up bringing out the sewing machine, most of the tools from her first class, a square template, and an iron.

"I'm about to teach you something, Miss Toss-out-perfectly-fine-fabric." I watched as she used the rotary cutter to cut a pentagon shape, sewed different scraps together around the pentagon's edges, and ironed after each seam. She made a point of using the ugly scraps until she had a large piece. Then she laid the square template on top and cut the whole thing into a perfect square.

She held the square out and looked it over approvingly. It was a jumble of mismatched florals, prints, and plaids. Nothing matched, yet somehow, it made a muddled kind of beautiful. All the ugly pieces blended in just fine, like a few bad memories tucked into an otherwise happy life.

She slid the template toward me. "Now, you give it a try."

First, I pulled a striped green seersucker for my center pentagon, put a piece of strawberry-print cotton on the longest side, and kept going until I had my own perfectly mixed-up square. Holly ran her hand over it.

"After my husband passed, I made a whole quilt out of his clothes. Even made a square using a pair of his boxers. I washed them, of course."

Holly winked, but her face turned serious. "How about you make more of these squares, and I figure out a way to work them into the border of my quilt for the contest? Deadline's tomorrow morning. If we want a shot at the prize money, we'll have to use the General." Holly patted the new sewing machine. "That's what I decided to name him." I laughed, and she handed me more scraps. My quilting display would have to wait.

23

Hook, Line, and Stinker

The Friday before Main Street Fest was loaded thick with worry. I'd spent the last few nights mulling over what I'd say to Momma and then praying the right words would be enough.

Abby's nerves were shot. She didn't even feel like fishing. We'd decided to paint one of her mom's step stools as a distraction; Abby's mom was so short, she carried around a lightweight collapsible stool to all major events. We'd chosen blue and were stenciling white stars all over it.

"Your mom is going to love this," I said.

"Speaking of. I can't believe I'm going to meet Brent Chisholm and your mom. What's she like?" Abby asked.

I inspected our work, and my stomach filled with flutters again. Every thought of Momma reminded me of my plan and what lay in store for me if it didn't work. Besides that, what was Momma like? I didn't even know how to answer.

"Busy," I said. This was the perfect time to tell Abby the whole truth, tell her that Momma was pressing me to move, and tell her that I didn't want to. But instead, I pointed to one of the stars. "Will you hand me the stencil? This one needs a touch-up."

Abby's mom walked out as I dabbed a second coat onto a star that really didn't need it to begin with. "Wow! I don't know why I didn't think of this before. Every mayor needs a patriotic step stool." She knelt down and joined us on the grass. "I've been thinking, it might be nice for you kids to say a few words before the concert tomorrow night. I can't tell you how proud it makes me to see you all so invested in your community." Her voice wobbled, tears welling in her eyes.

"Mom, come on. No more crying." Abby stood and gave her a quick hug before gently pushing her back in the direction of the house.

"She's been going on and on like that since she first found out about our idea. Don't freak out, but she wants us to start a youth action community service committee when school starts."

"YACS. We might need to rethink the name," I joked.

"We don't have to do it if you don't want to." She shrugged. "I mean, I'll be pretty busy with Junior Bassmasters."

I didn't even know if I'd be in Hope Springs when school started. But saying it out loud made moving feel more likely, so instead I said, "Sure. That'd be fun." She smiled, and I could barely look her in the eye.

"I have something to show you." She led me to their back porch. Stacked on a bench were boxes and boxes of baby food jars packed full of a brownish paste. "I got the idea from you—making something myself. I'm going to sell them at the Bassmasters booth tomorrow. What do you think?"

I picked up a jar and read the label: ABBY'S FAMOUS DIP BAIT: FRESHNESS NOT GUARANTEED.

"I almost went with 'Buy It—Hook, Line, and Stinker.' You're the expert. What do you think?"

"They're perfect," I said.

"I thought I'd sell some of the lures too." She held up a jar again. "I don't mean to brag, but this stuff could be a game changer." She lowered her voice to a whisper. "I'll tell you because you're my best friend: It's mostly blended hot dog wiener and some really stinky cheese. The stinkier, the better."

I laughed. "You'll sell out for sure."

Best friend. Those two words dropped right into my heart.

I left before sunset and walked my bike back rather than ride it—anything to stretch out the trip. With Nan and Wynn at home, there wasn't much alone time to think. The scratchy chirp of katydids filled the evening air. I kicked at the gravel, letting the dust cover my legs.

Best friend. The words repeated in my head over and over, a courage-chant for the rest of the evening. I hoped more than anything that I had the chance to go to school with Abby, to keep her as a best friend, to stay. But hoping so didn't make it so. I had to tell her the whole truth right away—or first thing in the morning at the latest.

24

Ready, Set, Rally

The morning of the rally, everybody met at our house, mostly because Brent Chisholm was expected to show up and no one could resist the chance to get an early, in-person peek at him. Miss Esther arrived with donuts and a new digital camera at six thirty in the morning. Wynn made pot after pot of coffee and tried hard to act as excited as everyone else.

Brent Chisholm's black tour bus rolled up just before nine. The bus stretched out over the whole length of our driveway. I stood in front of the window and watched, stiff with nerves, as most everyone else rushed out to the yard. Momma stepped out, a perfectly timed breeze gently tossing her curls, and I swear, Miss Esther clapped. Wynn stood next to me and said, "Well, I guess it's time we faced the music." He bumped my arm with his. "Get it?"

I rolled my eyes but gave him a quick hug. "Want to come out with me?"

"Nah. Go on," he said. "I'll come out in a minute."

Brent Chisholm strode off the bus looking like he'd stepped straight out of a country music video, pearl snaps and all. He was tanned and muscled, wore a black Stetson cowboy hat, and his chest made a guest appearance through a shirt with a few too many unfastened buttons. All the ladies seemed impressed beyond words. I noticed right away how he held Momma's hand for a split second before our guests mobbed him.

Wynn sneaked out the front door; he must have noticed the hand-holding too. Holly fanned herself, mouthy Miss Esther had nothing to say for once, and even Nan blushed like a schoolgirl when Brent shook her hand.

Brent sauntered up to me and said, "Jubilee, I've heard so much about you. I think what you and your friends have done here is awesome, and I'm happy to be a part of it." He pumped my hand like he expected to draw water, and then put his arm around Momma. Wynn shuffled around, hardly lifting his eyes from his freshly shined boots.

Brent Chisholm's big smile, put-together outfit, and ease with strangers didn't fool me for a hot minute—those were all sure signs of someone with a well-practiced set of Relocation Rules. But Momma smiled at him like he caused the sun to shine.

After all the introductions, Momma pulled me inside while Brent chatted and soaked up compliments. The parade started in a few hours, and the rally was scheduled to begin at three. One thing I knew was that, when people wanted to talk alone, it was usually something big.

She sat at our kitchen table and motioned for me to sit beside her.

"I've got some great news, Jubi. Brent's bought us a house in Dallas. When I say us, I mean you and me. And it's pretty as a dollhouse, sugar. Wait until you see it."

I didn't say anything. I couldn't. My mouth opened, closed, and opened again like a fish pulled from the pond and thrown on the bank.

Just like that? She expected me to move in with her without even talking to me about it first!

"Did Nan talk to you?" I asked.

"We talked the other night. But I thought I'd tell you the news myself. What do you think?" she asked. She twisted her hands into a bundle, bit her bottom lip, and shook her crossed legs. Momma was nervous. What I'd planned to say slipped away as soon as I saw she meant it. She really did want me.

"Momma, I don't know." I stared at Nan's kissing squirrel salt and pepper shakers. "What about Nan? What about Wynn?"

"Oh, I love Wynn like an older brother. He knows that." She didn't mention Nan and waited for my answer. Seemed to me Wynn and I had the same problem: Momma always thinking of us more as siblings, ready to take us in or wave us away at the drop of a hat—a black Stetson hat in Wynn's case.

"I already looked into private schools. Can you believe it? Private. Schools. You wouldn't have to worry about your outfit every day. And since the tour is still going, we could get someone to stay with us, someone young and fun, an au pair. Sounds fancy, right?" She laughed, but when I didn't, she turned serious. "Look, I'm great on stage, and I write great songs. I know I'm not as great in real life. But I'm your momma."

Again, I stayed silent, and Momma's smile faded even more. "Well, you think it over. Nan admitted all this moving had to stop and mentioned maybe moving closer to Dallas. We can talk about it more. I know you're not sold on the idea, but if you're going to start over, why not start over with me?" She clasped her hand over mine.

She hadn't listened to Nan at all. Or maybe she had but only heard what she wanted to.

I took a deep breath, readying myself to tell Momma the whole truth, when someone cleared their throat. Momma and I were so wrapped up in each other that neither of us noticed Abby standing in the doorway. "Didn't mean to interrupt," she said, her face blank.

"Abby, I was going to tell you—" I started, but she didn't let me finish before turning and racing out the door.

I ran right after her. By the time I caught up, she was already on her bike, about to take off.

"Abby, let me explain. I just couldn't find the right time," I said. "Besides, nothing's been decided yet."

"What were you going to do? Make me another stupid fish out of a toilet paper roll the day you left?" She rode off and yelled over her shoulder, "See you at the rally—if you don't up and move before then!"

25

The Right Thing

Nan, Wynn, and I went to the parade while Momma, Brent, and his crew went to do a sound check and set up. On the drive to town, I kept replaying my conversation with Momma. I hadn't given her the answer I meant to. In fact, I'd said I didn't know, which wasn't a bit right.

We pulled into a parking spot and got out. Nan hooked her arm through mine, and Wynn did the exact same thing on the other side. It was dorky, but just what I needed. I knew exactly where I wanted to be and who I wanted to be with. We walked like that all the way to the front of the Fabric Barn.

Kids ran toward Main Street, shrieking with laughter while their parents chased after them. Wynn carried three folded lawn chairs with his free arm and set them up on the sidewalk in front of the Fabric Barn. Abby's family would settle in front of the One Stop, and I made myself not look over.

Holly came out to say hi. Wynn stood. "Have a seat," he said, offering his chair.

"I wish I could," she said. "Believe it or not, I've got a few customers. I'll help them, lock the door, and then join you."

When she returned, she gave me quick kiss on the head. The shock of her greetings and fare-wells had worn off. I'd gotten used to hugs and pecks.

As the parade music began, I hardly talked and no one seemed to notice. Over the past few days, I'd been growing this small bit of hope, let-ting it build up little by little like yarn wrapped from a skein. Now with Abby mad at me, I felt it unraveling. I'd made such a mess of the whole living with Momma situation. How could I possibly fix things?

A few families lined the street in front of us with a herd of children who attacked thrown candy like a pack of wolves. The floats were mostly flatbeds full of metal folding chairs holding people from different clubs—except the Springer Swingers, square dancers who used their flatbed to put on a show, and the Kiwanis club, whose members dressed like clowns and rode around on four-wheelers. A clown zoomed by and waved right at me, his big rainbow wig blowing in the wind, and then he reached into a fanny pack, pulled out a handful of candy, and threw it.

"Look." I nudged Wynn and Nan. "They're actually wearing clown wigs and fanny packs."

They laughed, but I couldn't bring myself back to happy. I went ahead and looked over at the One Stop. Harrison and Garfield both waved. Abby didn't. But I remembered what she'd said on our first trip to the pond, about the people of Hope

Springs being what made the place special. As I waved back to her little brothers, I had an idea that would take all the courage I could muster.

When I got back home, I collected my supplies for the rally. Wynn knocked on my doorframe and stuck his head in. "I think your momma will come around. But you're going to have to put all your cards on the table," he said. "If you don't come right out and say it, she'll be able to tell herself she didn't know how you really felt." He gave me a sad smile. "Believe me, I know."

I nodded. If he never told Momma how he felt, she could move on like it didn't matter, like *he* didn't matter. I guess Momma was pretty good at moving on too. If ever there was a time for working up the courage to tell the whole truth, it was now.

So much hovered over me that, by the time we got to Griggs' Rigs Racing, I was almost sorry I'd ever thought up the rally to begin with. But then I saw the tracks all decorated with colorful pennant banners and a motor revved, nearly matching the speed of my heartbeat. We'd done it.

The booths Colton and his brothers built lined the fairway, already drawing a crowd. And things weren't supposed to start for another half hour. Even the Springer Swingers were there, still in their dancing outfits.

I left Wynn and Nan and searched for Abby's mom. I found her shaking hands by Miss Esther's homemade jams and jellies booth.

"Mrs. Standridge, can I talk to you for a second?" I asked.

"Call me Myrna." She stepped to the back of the booth and I followed. "Listen, honey, I know you and Abby had some kind of argument. You two will work it out. I don't want to get in the middle."

"I'll try to talk to Abby, but I wanted to ask you something else. I want to talk before the concert, right before Arletta, but I want to make sure what I have to say is okay with you." I outlined my speech, she listened, nodded, and rubbed her chin in true mayoral style.

"Let me think about it for a bit, and I'll come find you at your craft table," she said when I'd finished explaining.

The kids' craft table had been a good idea for three reasons: It kept me busy and distracted, I got to spend some time with Garfield and Harrison, and Holly was at the Fabric Barn booth right next to me. My pint-sized group made monster faces on tennis balls. I cut the balls halfway across the middle for the mouth, and then with a squeeze, they opened up to hold coins. All the kids hoped they'd win the wishing penny raffle after making their very own monster coin purses. When Abby's mom came to pick up the twins she said, "Go ahead. It's worth it."

Abby's booth was across the fairway from mine. She didn't have to try to avoid me; she was too busy. The line for her lures and dip bait was never fewer than twenty people deep. Even though we were both swamped, I caught her looking my way a few times.

As I packed away my supplies before the concert started, Colton walked over with a boy about a foot taller. Most people had cleared out, drifting to the stage. The tall boy gave Colton a push in my direction, while I tried to act like I wasn't watching.

"That's one of my brothers. Truitt, the tall one," Colton said.

I smiled, but all I could think of was what I planned to say in front of a crowd of people and if Abby would ever forgive me. Asking Arletta Paisley a question on her show was big, like jumping over a deep ravine to get to the other side, but what I was about to do was like leaping off a cliff with no other side in sight.

"So, your mom and Brent are setting up," he said. "She said my stage was 'cute as a bug's ear,' but they needed a 'smidgen' more space." He used finger quotes. "Also said you might be moving soon."

How could she tell Colton? I slammed my boxes on the table. Beads and sequins scattered, and tennis balls bounced in all directions. A hot, tight feeling crept up my throat. I knelt down and crawled under my table, pretending to pick up supplies, just in time to hide the first tears that sneaked down my cheeks. As I wiped at my face, Colton's head leaned down and then he crouched beside me, quietly picking googly eyes out of the dirt.

"I'm sorry," I said. "I should've told Abby and you too. But it's not for sure. My mom...she doesn't even really know me. But I'm about to do something that might help, if it doesn't scare me to death first." I started to stand but stopped when I noticed Colton smiling at me.

"What are you smiling at?" I picked up a few tennis balls and stuffed them into my bag.

"Not knowing you—it's her loss." He handed me a tennis ball. Colton might be stingy with words sometimes, but he sure chose the right ones when it counted. We walked over to the stage together, his hand holding mine.

"I'm nervous," I admitted.

"You can do it," he said without even knowing my plan. "Whatever it is. You can do it." He smiled so big that I believed him—for three of the five steps up to the stage, I totally believed him.

There were hundreds of people by now, a sea of hats and hairdos. Momma and Brent were to the side of the stage, and Arletta Paisley stood right next to my mom. Abby's mom shook each of their hands before walking out to the mic stand, and instead of adjusting the microphone to a lower setting, she used the step stool Abby and I painted.

"I know Brent Chisholm and Lexie Kirk are about to play, but let's be honest, the real reason we're all here is to see who wins this quilt contest. Am I right?" A few laughs and hoots answered her. "Despite the short notice, we had more than fifty entries. And the winner is... owner of the Fabric Barn, Holly Paine!"

Holly took the stage with Rayburn trotting close behind wearing a red bandanna, and my hands burned from clapping so hard. The quilt was rolled out on a display rack used for hanging clothes. Stitched in the center was the well from the town's square; above it, Holly had embroidered the words *Hope Springs Eternal* and below, *A treasure worth more than gold.* Around the edge were the squares we'd made together from scraps left by the people of Hope Springs—every print and color imaginable, a real mismatched jumble that together looked perfect.

Holly accepted an envelope from Abby's mom and handed it right back.

"Thank you, Mayor. Now I'd like to take my winnings and donate them to the Downtown Revitalization Fund. And I'd like to thank my business partner, Jubilee Johnson, for all her help and inspiring ideas." The applause and yelling went on for a few minutes, and I smiled as my cheeks warmed from the unexpected attention.

"The judges felt that Holly's quilt embodied the spirit of Hope Springs. And I personally think this gesture"—Abby's mom held up the envelope—"does as well. We are a community that rallies together, that supports each other. All of you being here shows we can do a lot more than hope, when we work together." The crowd erupted, and my voice joined the shouts. "Before we start, we have a special guest who would like to say a few words."

Arletta took a few steps forward, but Abby's mom stopped her with a hand and motioned for me. I walked past Arletta, making sure not to meet her eyes. One misstep and I might lose my nerve. It wasn't until I got close to the microphone that I realized I was humming "Row, Row, Row Your Boat."

My insides felt like they'd up and turned into fireflies. I took a deep breath and smelled fresh hay bales and the pine planks used for the stage, and I thought I even caught a whiff of the pond—scents that alone wouldn't have been anything special, but together were "just right" perfect.

26

A Wishing Penny

Not that long ago, I went to the wishing well downtown. Nan and I haven't lived here long, and we'd been searching for our 'just right' place for a while. When I first got to town, I almost wished for Hope Springs to be that perfect place for us. But really, I moved here for one reason only. Because it was Arletta Paisley's hometown."

The audience clapped politely. I fought to steady my voice, and continued.

"I thought everything Arletta Paisley did was

pure gold. One thing I lived by was her saying 'Nothing says you care like a handmade gift.' But lately, I've been around a lot of people who care, and giving gifts doesn't have much to do with it. Nothing says you care like spending time with your friends, family, and neighbors."

Abby's face in the crowd caught my attention, and she gave me a smile that boosted my courage.

"I had the honor of meeting Ms. Paisley backstage at her show." I paused and looked at Arletta then. She gave a nervous smile to the smattering of applause. "She told me if I had any sense, I'd leave Hope Springs as soon as I could, just like she did. But of all the places I've lived, I've been the happiest here. I got a job, helped with this rally, and made a few best friends that I hope I can keep.

"I've decided there aren't really any perfect places, but Hope Springs is close. If you ask me, I got what I wished for, even if it was only for a little while. I got a home."

Then I focused on Momma. I dug deep and

hoped my eyes told her how sorry I was that my home wasn't with her. Her smile had fallen, but I saw Brent reach for her hand.

"And I just wanted to say thank you to everyone here who had a part in that. I don't want SmartMart to fail. Really, I don't. But with my whole heart, I don't want Hope Springs to either."

Abby's mom walked up and circled her arm around my waist. There was so much chaos from the audience, it was a long while before she could talk again.

"And now we have Ms. Arletta Paisley herself here to say a few words and kick off the big event." Abby's mom held an open arm out to welcome Arletta to the microphone. I stood right there and looked my ex-idol straight in the face. Her high-heeled cowboy boots hadn't taken two steps before the first boo came, low and clear. Then a few more boos joined in, and more until the crowd sounded like a herd of cattle.

Arletta's smile vanished, and she stared at me with her true face. All the makeup in the world couldn't have covered up the ugliness in that look. That's when I noticed several flashes and looked out to see a few people crouched around the stage with cameras, and some in the audience were recording the whole thing with their phones. Arletta must have seen the same thing because she turned, showed her toothpaste commercial smile, and waved to the crowd.

She cleared her throat, the microphone screeched, and she shot a look to the sound booth. I wished toe-achingly hard that she'd fall off the stage and land face-first in the mud. She didn't. She cleared her throat again and started speaking.

"Hope Springs has always been special to me. My time here shaped me in ways that to this day contribute to my success, and for that, I'm very grateful to this community." There were still a few boos, but not nearly as many.

"I often talk about being from here, but something I don't often talk about is how I ended up here." Arletta paused to soak up the silence. I swear her eyes glistened with tears. Every mouth shut, and not a single ear wasn't listening.

"My mother raised me by herself. We moved here because a friend of a friend promised my mother a job that fell through on our second day in town. Preacher Fleming arranged for us to stay with a widow who owned a large house and rented out rooms. Mrs. Prudence Hatley let us live with her for months and wouldn't take a penny in rent while my mother looked for work.

"Mrs. Hatley taught me to sew, knit, and crochet. I owe that woman more than just my career. I'm sure a few of you knew her. She passed a while back, but it's in her honor that I'd like to donate twenty-five thousand dollars to the Hope Springs Downtown Revitalization Fund."

At first, only a few claps rang through the crowd, but after a few seconds, the people sitting on hay bales and blankets stood, applauding and hollering. Arletta Paisley got a standing ovation. Far from the muddy face-plant I'd been picturing.

Abby's mom tightened her arm around me and whispered, "Well, you gave her a piece, and we still get that donation." She was a politician with a big heart, but still a politician.

I wasn't sure if Arletta had won. She sure hadn't lost.

Staring out into the crowd, I knew I hadn't lost either. Nan and Wynn stood in the front row, Holly smiled up at me, Abby's dad towered above everyone with Garfield on his shoulders and Harrison holding his hand, and Abby and Colton were there beside them. Abby was right. The best thing about Hope Springs was the people. I'd never felt a part of something so special.

After the clapping died down, Arletta smiled for a few photos. Then she said, "Okay, folks. It's time for what we've all been waiting for. Lexie Kirk and Brent Chisholm!"

As Momma took the stage, she gave me a true hug and whispered, "I'm so proud of you, sweetheart."

I nodded and said, "Me too."

Arletta rushed past us in a flurry of blonde hair and denim. For once, I didn't feel like pulling away from Momma. I hugged her right back. I far preferred my real momma.

As I turned and neared the steps, Abby and Colton rushed the stage and tackled me in a hug that felt better than just about anything. We stood together, our trio at the corner of the stage, and listened as a steel guitar started off the first song.

Momma and Brent really tore it up. Momma sang three songs all on her own before the duet with Brent. Then she sang backup while he sang hits from all his albums, but he had her stand right beside him. I was so proud, I felt like telling everyone around that that lady up on stage was my momma, but I also thanked my stars they didn't sing that dang donut song.

Afterward, we went to my house, and Abby's dad brought all the leftovers from the One Stop booth to set up in our yard. Brent, Momma, Nan, Wynn, Holly, Miss Esther, and Abby's family all managed to squeeze onto our patch of lawn together. Everybody ate and laughed and made toasts. It was what Thanksgiving dinner should be like, but never had been. Happiness seemed to float on the breeze, but I had one more cliff to climb.

While everyone laughed and carried on in the front yard, I sneaked around, grabbed Momma and Nan, and dragged them into the house.

"Could you both sit down?" I asked. We all scooted around our tiny table with our knees almost touching. "Nan, I love you. But I don't want to keep moving all the time. In fact, I don't think I want to ever move again." Momma crossed her arms, the glimmer of an I-told-you-so smile creeping across her lips. "And, Momma, I can't even picture living with you. We hardly know each other." From the look on Momma's face, the whole truth was as hard for her to hear as it was for me to say. "Though I'd like that to change."

Wynn still hadn't fastened the cabinet doors back on, and all the contents of the shelves were visible. I felt the same way. Nan and Momma were about to see all I had to show. All my doors were off.

"Momma," I took her letter from my pocket,

unfolded it, and slid it over to her, "you remember writing this?"

She glanced down, her eyes filled, and she nodded.

"You were at the rally. You've met all my friends and have seen how happy I am here with Nan and Wynn. This place, Hope Springs, this is where I sing."

Momma leaned her head down and nodded. "I missed my chance, didn't I?" she asked.

"Maybe you missed one chance. But luckily you don't get just one," I said.

Nan cleared her throat. "I'd like to say something too. I justified moving us by telling myself it was to protect Jubilee. I thought her life had already been tough enough. So anytime there was trouble, I packed us up. But if I'm honest, I did it to protect myself too," she said. "And to keep everyone at a distance. After I'd been left by my husband and son, I guess I decided I'd do all the leaving from then on."

"Nan—" I started, but she stopped me.

"I want you to have what's best. 'Hearts have windows, but mine has doors a painful past has closed.' Travis Tritt." Nan looked at Momma. "I think we might all suffer from the same problem, Alexandra. It's time to open up our hearts and let a few more people in. I've shut you out, and that wasn't right." Nan reached one hand out to me and the other out to Momma.

Momma sat and stared at Nan's hand. She sniffed, wiped a tear away, and then took it. She held her other hand out to me, and we sat holding hands in a ring. Me, Momma, and Nan. If I hadn't been a part of that little circle, I'd never have believed it was possible.

"I don't understand it, but if you want to stay here, I'll visit more often. Dallas is only a few hours away," Momma said.

"I can stay?" I asked.

She looked at Nan and nodded. "You can stay," they said together.

I screamed the loudest hooray and danced around the kitchen like a fool. Momma managed a tight smile. Nan hopped up faster than she'd moved all month, put both arms around me, and squeezed.

"I think it's time we come up with some Staying Put Procedures," she whispered. I could only nod. Momma stood too, wiped a few tears from her cheeks, and we all walked back out together.

Everybody stayed until around midnight when Nan made such a show of yawning, they took the hint and started heading out. For the first time, Momma was the last person to leave. Brent waited in the tour bus while she said goodbye.

"You call me soon," Momma said. She smoothed my hair. "I love you, you know." I nodded, and for the first time ever, I believed her.

I turned and looked at our little rental house lit up by a pale moon. First days I was used to, but a home...a home was a whole new project.

27

Staying Put Procedure Number 1

By the time school started in August, Nan and I had done a heaping handful of hard things. Nan had even gone on a date and afterward, though I suspected she thought about the maps, she didn't mention them once. She'd worked a full month at the nursing home without the normal complaints, she and Miss Esther were regulars at ladies' night bingo, and she went to Holly's classes once a week. And we bought a couch. A big, overstuffed, almost impossible to move couch. It took Colton and two of his brothers to unload it and carry it into our house.

"What about above your bed?" Abby asked. She held one corner of the Dresden plate quilt I'd recently finished. Each square had a plain white background, but in the center was a pinwheel-shaped flower, every petal a different colored fabric. I'd used a few of Nan's old black denim shirts, some of Abby's shorts, plenty of vintage prints from Holly, the skirt Momma wore to the rally concert, a bright John Deere–green cotton, some embroidered patches here and there—a donation from Wynn's collection of Western shirts—and even a few of Rayburn's well-washed bandannas. Nan had given me one of my daddy's shirts, but I couldn't bear to cut it up. Each piece in the quilt was special. Just a glance at it made me want to run my fingers across the stitches.

"Hmmm. I'm not so sure I want it hanging over my head," I said.

Abby and I rotated houses for sleepovers almost every weekend. We weren't in the same class, but she was right across the hall. School didn't give us enough time to visit, so Abby lifted her talking ban while fishing. And we always had a lot to talk about. She still caught a lot of fish, a fact I wasn't about to mention. I even snagged my first fish, a tiny bluegill. The photo Colton took that day sits in a frame on my nightstand—all three of us smashed together right in the middle of a laugh.

Miss Esther came out of retirement to train the new middle school librarian, and she'd been glaring into classrooms and eyeballing teachers for weeks. Holly also asked Abby and me to start a quilting club at school, and she provided all the fabric. So far, we had twelve kids signed up.

Holly started our first quilting club meeting with what she called "The History of American Quilt Making." She told us how, long ago, paper was scarce so women cut up old letters and newspaper articles to make patterns, then stuffed the paper between the quilt layers for extra insulation.

The next meeting, I brought in some of Momma's letters cut into a Dresden plate pattern.

Dresden plate quilts were also called friendship rings, grandmother's sunburst, and sunflower quilts. I didn't feel right throwing the leftover letters away or keeping them under my bed again; so I placed them inside the quilt along with the batting just like they did in the old days. Abby helped me during school, and Holly helped me after. Momma had quit writing letters and I was done letting them follow me around, but I wasn't sure I wanted to sleep under them every night.

Letting go of the letters was easier than getting close to Momma, but so far, she'd kept her promise. She'd visited twice, and I had plans to spend the weekend with her and Brent once their tour wrapped up. When I'd searched for Ernest Hemingway quotes to persuade Nan to stay in Hope Springs, I'd come across one I was trying my hardest to believe in: "The best way to find out if you can trust somebody is to trust them."

"Well, what about in your crafting room? Right above the sewing table," Abby asked.

"Perfect!" We made our way down the hall. Just then, Wynn appeared, still wearing his uniform from working at the new Wreck O Mend, an auto repair shop in the SmartMart center. According to the newspaper, SmartMart's grand opening was a big old dud. It was still there, and though Nan and I were tempted, we hadn't stepped foot inside.

Wynn came over every Saturday for dinner. Now that he'd moved out, I missed him, but on the bright side, I did have my crafting room back.

I rushed over to help him with the groceries and he held a finger to his lips and whispered, "Help me set some things up. I'm going to trick Nan into a cooking lesson." We pulled out a loaf pan and a cookie sheet and set all the ingredients on the counter.

Nan poked her head in and said, "Well, you're here early."

"Thought I'd make us my mother's famous meatloaf." Wynn made a big show of dropping the packaged ground beef in the sink, and then both pans hit the floor.

"What's going on with you?" Nan asked.

"Oh, I got a bit of a burn on my hand at the

shop today." He held up his bandaged hand and sent me a quick wink.

"You want me to look at it?" she asked.

"No, it'll be fine," he said. "But I could use a hand in the kitchen."

For the next half hour, Nan banged around and said at least half a dozen almost-swears. Abby and I sneaked to the door as she yelled, "Spiny lumpsucker!" and waved her fingers around, dripping egg yolk on the floor before dashing over to the sink.

"Is Nan going to be all right?" Abby whispered.

I nodded.

"Oh, fishsticks and fuzzbuckets!" Nan hollered.

"We'll pick the eggshells out. There's not many in there," Wynn said.

"We're going for a quick bike ride!" I grabbed Abby by the arm and pulled her out the door. "Or a long one," I whispered.

"Be back here in thirty minutes for dinner!" Nan yelled. "Wynn, is this *broccoli*?"

Wynn met us at the door. "Probably more like an hour," he said. "And no sneaking over to Abby's for dinner," he added like he'd read my mind.

Abby and I stepped onto the porch with the August evening sun lowering and lighting the belly of clouds in pink and orange neon. Wynn's sunflowers from early in the summer still stood tall in our front beds. There on my porch with my best friend, everything felt just right, from top to bottom, through and through just right.

"Colton's working at the track. Want to ride over and say hi?" I asked.

"Sure. Race you?" Abby asked, already crouched to a ready stance and eyeing our bikes. I nodded, certain we'd race a short while before slowing down to ride side by side.

"Ready, set—" Abby started to count down, and I took off. "Cheater!" she yelled.

We ran out in my yard, where Wynn's shiny red truck sat next to our dusty hatchback and Abby's bike lay beside my carefully propped up new-old bike. It reminded me of how lonesome our apartment complex parking lots used to be. Even though those lots were full of cars, we didn't really know anyone, never let anyone get close to us. But I'd learned the more I loved didn't have to mean the more I had to lose. Love didn't work like anything else in the world—the more I gave away, the more I got back.

My life was turning out a lot like one of Holly's scrap quilt squares. Some ugly patches mixed in here and there but, overall, it was shaping up to look like a mismatched jumble of better than perfect.

ACKNOWLEDGMENTS

I consider myself incredibly lucky to have so many people to thank. This book would not exist if it weren't for the help of others.

First and foremost, thank you, Mom and Dad, for making sure stories and books were a part of every day from the very beginning.

Thank you to my sisters, Katie and Lauren; our childhood has supplied me with endless material.

Thank you to my early readers, Chris Chavis, Siva Ramakrishnan, Traci Tullius, Katrina Muir, Peggy Wolf, and again, Mom—without you all, I never would've had the courage to try.

Thank you to my critique partners, Gigi Collins, Tisha Hamilton, Joanne Kelleher, Ellen Mulholland, and especially Collomia Charles and Mary Park, who were the first to set eyes on this story many years ago.

➤➤➤ ACKNOWLEDGMENTS ◄◄◄

Thank you to Nicole Rudick for good advice whenever I needed it.

Thank you to my fierce and talented agent, Kaitlyn Johnson, whose eye for detail and quick wit make my stories so much better.

Thank you to my amazing editor, Samantha Gentry, whose feedback turned this into a story I'm truly proud of, and who treated this book with such care that I suspect she may love it as much as I do.

Thanks to the entire team at Little, Brown Books for Young Readers.

Thank you to Oriol Vidal and Karina Granda for creating a cover that brought Jubilee and her story to life.

Thank you to all the teachers and caregivers who look after and teach my children.

And finally, thank you to my family who put up with me daily but really went all out during my edits. Chris, Owen, Sam, and Henry, I love you all so much.

Lee Seidenberg Photography

Jaime Berry is a native of rural Oklahoma. After years with two small boys in a too-small Brooklyn apartment, Jaime and her husband moved to the wilds of suburban New Jersey and added another boy and a dog to the mix. There, they live in a Victorian house that, despite slowly falling apart, they all love. And where telling, reading, and writing stories takes up most of her day. *Hope Springs* is Jaime's debut novel. She invites you to visit her at jaimeberryauthor.com or on Twitter @jaime_berry3.